The Book of the Ghost

Also by Eric R. Asher

Keep track of Eric's new releases by receiving an email on release day. It's fast and easy to sign up for Eric's mailing list, and you'll also get an ebook copy of the subscriber exclusive anthology, *Whispers of War*.

Go here to get started: www.ericrasher.com

The Steamborn Trilogy:

Steamborn

Steamforged

Steamsworn

The Vesik Series:

(Recommended for Ages 17+)

Days Gone Bad

Wolves and the River of Stone

Winter's Demon

This Broken World

Destroyer Rising

Rattle the Bones

Witch Queen's War

Forgotten Ghosts

The Book of the Ghost

The Book of the Claw*

The Book of the Sea*

The Book of the Staff*

The Book of the Rune*

The Book of the Sails*
The Book of the Wing*
The Book of the Blade*
The Book of the Fang*
The Book of the Reaper*

The Vesik Series Box Sets

Box Set One (Books 1-3)
Box Set Two (Books 4-6)
Box Set Three (Books 7-8)
Box Set Four: The Books of the Dead Part 1 (Coming in 2020)*
Box Set Five: The Books of the Dead Part 2 (Coming in 2020)*

Mason Dixon – Monster Hunter:

Episode One
Episode Two
Episode Three

*Want to receive an email when one of Eric's books releases? Sign up for Eric's mailing list.
www.ericrasher.com

The Book of
the Ghost

Eric R. Asher

Edited by Laura Matheson
Cover typography by Indie Solutions by Murphy Rae
Cover design ©Phatpuppyart.com – Claudia McKinney

Author's Note

The Books of the Dead start here! If you're asking yourself, "Self, what are The Books of the Dead and who is this Vesik fellow?" then you may not have read the previous books in the Vesik series.

While I'm not one to judge, I've included an excerpt from Days Gone Bad, the first book—aka that one book with the exploding pigeons. And no, my 1-star reviewer friend, I do not condone the blowing up of pigeons in real life.

Now that you know, please don't summon the legions of the dead to pummel me because *The Book of the Ghost* ends around the 90% mark. If you think I write slow now, just wait until I have to do it while fending off Chuck the vampire.

Enough of that. Strap in for a crazy ride, because we have a new installment of The Books of the Dead launching almost every month for a solid year. Now excuse me while I get a chimichanga.

Thanks for the support!
Eric

Someone asked if I was going to apologize for that last cliffhanger, but then – oh look my chimichanga is ready!

CHAPTER ONE

Vicky clung to the spikes on Jasper's back as they soared over the carnage of Falias. Tears threatened the corners of her eyes as Jasper rocketed toward the wooden platform below, leaving Damian's colossal form behind. She'd find a way to save him, but for now their allies needed all the help they could get.

And Damian had become the biggest threat to every soul on that battlefield. Shadows and skeletons erupted around his form, lashing out to swallow allies and enemies alike into a terrible darkness.

The figures below, who so recently looked like dots upon a scorched plain, resolved into the scrambling forces of the Obsidian Inn. The dark-touched vampires engaged them in pockets, but whatever Damian had become was cutting people down without bias.

A black blur in Vicky's periphery caught her attention. A soulsword flashed to life in her right hand, the blade a fiery and vibrant gold. Jasper tried to roll away from the incoming vampire, but as agile as the dragon was, he couldn't dodge the attack. It mattered little. Vicky let the anger rise through her body until her aura sang with the violence of a thousand murdered souls.

One vicious slash sent the dark-touched reeling with a molten wound in its helmet. Jasper followed it down to where it crashed onto a wide wooden platform that held three massive stakes. This was supposed to be a place of execution, and Liam, Lochlan, and Enda were each tied to one of the stakes, waiting to meet their fate. Vicky hopped off Jasper's back as the dragon took to incinerating the dark-touched vampire beneath his claws.

Vicky's heart leapt when a squadron of furry hunched forms crashed through the line of Nudd's fairies. She'd know Caroline's wolf form anywhere. The pale line of fur etched down the left side of the werewolf's neck looked more like the pinstripe of an old car than the ancient bayonet wound Vicky knew it to be.

The clash at Gettysburg rose up in Vicky's memories, trying to take her out of the moment, trying to drag her back down into a darkness she'd fought for years to escape. The shadow of the leviathans, and Ezekiel, and the Old Man tried to smother the light from her mind, but she'd seen worse. Lived through worse.

The battle below came back into sharp relief as she stuffed those thoughts deep into the back of her mind. Jasper's scales were rocky beneath the soles of her boots when she mounted the beast once more. She swung her left leg over his spines and held on with one hand, waiting for his wings to thrust them into the sky once more, and at the peak of his ascent, she let go.

"Everyone dies," she whispered to herself as the wind whipped through her hair. "But not today."

The skies looked as clear as the targets below her, but she'd been mistaken. One second she'd been soaring above Falias in a mad dive, and the next a brutal impact sent the world spinning around her. She caught the glint of a stained armor before she realized what had hit her. An owl knight kicked her away, sending her reeling into a brawl among the were-wolves. Vicky grunted as she bounced off her side and rolled to a stop.

She took two deep breaths and climbed back to her feet.

"Little one!" Wahya roared, his golden fur rippling as he stood high on his hind legs, only to wrap his muscled form around a fairy before sending wings and dust and blood in three different directions. The werewolf grinned as he bounded along beside her.

Wahya felt like home, felt like he had more of a

connection to the Burning Lands than the other wolves, like she'd had with the Ghost Pack. Hugh felt like that too sometimes. As she impaled a distracted owl knight, Vicky wondered if the comfort she found in some of the wolves was because of the bond she shared with Damian and the Ghost Pack. Darkness seeped into the edges of her vision as the grief of losing Carter and Maggie welled up once more.

"Get to Enda and the others," Caroline growled. She turned and snapped the spine of one of the weird skeletons. "Get them out of here!"

Vicky glanced farther down the platform as she spun, slashing through the skeleton Caroline had broken in half. And what had been the skeleton from the shadows crumbled to ash between the werewolf's claws. The guards started to flee. Nudd's own people started to flee.

Liam pulled at his bonds as Vicky closed on him.

"I've got you," Vicky said. But before she could so much as slash the bonds from his wrists, Liam protested.

"Get my parents first. They're worse off than me. Untie them first."

Vicky hesitated for only a moment. As much as her instinct was to save the child first, she remembered what it was like to have people not listen to her, as if the fact that she was young discredited all of her experience.

Liam pulled at his bonds again even as Vicky rushed a few steps to Lochlan's side. The old Fae was far worse for wear. A dozen tiny gashes revealed a kind of torture Vicky couldn't comprehend. Dried blood had crusted around the fairy's eyes, and he barely protested when she grabbed his wrists and slashed his bonds away with her soulsword.

"Get Enda!" Vicky shouted as Wahya came into her view.

Wahya eyed Liam before reaching out a golden claw and severing Enda's bonds. Enda slumped into the golden werewolf's arms.

"Is she…" Liam started, but his voice choked off into a cry.

"She will live," Wahya said. "We only need a healer. And we have many."

Both of Liam's parents were still breathing, and the fact their flesh hadn't been siphoned away into the ley lines was a good sign, but Vicky kept that thought to herself. Wahya snapped Liam's bonds with his free hand, and though he reached for the boy, Liam refused, instead picking up a bloodied sword from the platform and squaring off against the skeletons that rode from the shadows.

"What is that thing?" Caroline asked, following Liam's line of sight up into the mass of skeletal riders surrounding the jackal-headed obsidian colossus.

Jasper unleashed a blue barrel of flame, casting the area around them into an eerie light. Before Vicky could respond to Caroline's question, the werewolf had already engaged with another fairy. Vicky slid around the battling pair, neatly severing the fairy's head while it was distracted by the werewolf. Even as she felt some relief as the body collapsed and started to fade into the ley lines, she saw more of the ghosts from the corner of her eye. They weren't calm sentinels anymore. They were moving of their own accord. While some of them meandered aimlessly, Vicky shivered as she realized the others were following the shadows of the vampires and Damian.

"You may be asking yourself what that thing is," Wahya said. "But the pressing question in my mind is how do we kill it?"

"You can't," Vicky said, even as Enda raised a hand to her chest in agreement of Wahya's assessment.

"I've killed a great many things that people said couldn't be killed," Caroline said. "I'm sure it can die."

"You don't understand," Vicky said. "That thing is Damian. You can't kill him."

Whatever Caroline had been about to say died on

her tongue. Her lips curled back as the golden sunburst of her eyes narrowed. Wahya, standing on his hind legs, almost folded in on himself as he lowered to all fours. His shoulders sagged, and he stared up at the colossus in the distance before returning his gaze to Vicky.

"How?" the golden werewolf asked. His voice was quiet, but Vicky could still hear him clearly over the distant battle.

"Nudd," Vicky said, and the name tasted like ash on her tongue. She hadn't fought so long and so hard to lose her friends like this. Dying had been terrible, but it had given her experience. The thought of Damian becoming that thing, and realizing that the end of him was the end of Sam, felt so much worse than knowing her own life was at risk. But she wasn't dead yet, and as long as her blades could still draw blood, she wouldn't stop.

"We have to get to the Morrigan," Caroline said. "Get her to retreat. At least pull back the forces closing on Damian."

Wahya rolled his shoulders forward. "It may not buy her enough time."

"The only other choice is to kill him." Caroline met Wahya's gaze.

Vicky looked at the Caroline. "If we kill him Sam

dies too."

"And you," Wahya said, turning his eyes to her.

Vicky shrugged. "I've died before. It's nothing new." The words might have sounded flippant coming out of the teenager's mouth, but that was the point. She hoped it would mask the uncertainty in her mind, the fear of dying she tried to hide from her friends. And the anxiety in her chest.

"Little one," Wahya said. "You need not hide your fears from us."

Vicky grimaced and lit a soulsword as another of the dark-touched vampires closed on their position. "Later," was all she said before she dove back into the fray. But even as Vicky engaged with their enemy, all she could see were Wahya's sad golden eyes looking down on her with something that was far too close to pity.

Pity was something she didn't need. If she'd learned anything from her years running with the Ghost Pack, it was how to be strong when the world around you crumbled to dust. She hadn't felt helpless in a long time, and she'd never be helpless again. Anger flowed through her like a torch, and the soulsword in her hand condensed into a beacon of golden light. Skeletons collapsed at a lick from her golden blade. And this dark-touched would fall like all the rest.

CHAPTER TWO

VICKY LOST HERSELF to the chaos of battle. She let the soulsword fade and retract from the armor of the dead Fae at her feet. Even as the knight she'd slayed screamed in his death throes, she watched in exhaustion as a line of ghosts marched, trailing the path of destruction Damian had carved through Falias. They moved as one, like solemn horses leading a funeral hearse, and the sight set Vicky's nerves on edge. All but one of the ghosts moved in tandem.

She eyed that one stray ghost, an old Civil War jacket wrapped around his shoulders as his gaze wandered left to where the werewolves engaged the vampires. The ghost's attention would be drawn back to the colossus, only to once more turn back toward the battle. Each step he took showed hesitation, and the oddity drew Vicky to him.

She hurried to the ghost, carefully sidestepping a pool of gravemaker flesh that boiled and slithered through the matted grass as it followed him.

"Can you hear me?" Vicky asked.

For a moment the ghost just stared up at the colossus, but his brow furrowed and his eyes turned toward Vicky. She'd seen enough ghosts in her time to know when there wasn't much left, when the thoughts of whoever they'd been had essentially become a video on a looped playback. This man was different. A golden glow sat behind his pupils.

Vicky reached out without thinking, and screeched when the vision overtook her.

She saw the soldier gunned down at a funeral. Saw the guitar fall from his hands and crash to the grass beneath them. Saw the Confederate, only a boy himself, howling mad over the dying musician. He screamed something about killing his brother, but Vicky's eyes were all on the green man lumbering out of the woods behind the boy. It was over in a flash. One moment a human, the next a pulped mass of flesh beneath a wrecking ball of wood and branches.

The green man crouched at the dying musician's side, and while Vicky couldn't make out the words, she could see the shadow beside them. The leather jacket, jeans, and the silver eyes of a necromancer.

The connection broke and Vicky collapsed to a knee. She gasped for breath as her vision dimmed. But this was no time to pass out. She looked behind her, horrified to see how far she'd run from the werewolves, from her only friends in this hellscape, before encountering the ghost. She limped toward them, stumbling and jogging as best she could before her foot caught on the empty armor of the Fae that had crumbled to the ground. She saw the soldier watching her as her vision finally gave out and a gentle paw lifted her into a werewolf's arms.

CHAPTER THREE

THE FIRST THING to come back to him was his name. Terrence. Musician, soldier in the Union Army, and buried at Greenville above the Black River. But though he'd called Greenville home for over a hundred and fifty years, the place he stood now was nowhere near it.

Memories of the conversations he'd had with Dirge and the man called Damian Vesik clawed their way to the surface of his mind. Even as something drew him toward the colossus in the distance, a golden light swelled in his vision, as if backlighting the world around him. He watched the werewolf, a massive golden hulk, so gently lift that girl from the earth. Whatever she'd done, she'd given him back some part of himself. She'd given him a light, a filter, that let him see nearby souls so clearly. But behind the crash of magicks and the screams of the dying, a voice whispered to him. It wasn't a seductive temptation like the cloying force pulling him toward that colossus. It was a cry for help.

"Only you. You're the only one."

"Only one who what?" Terrence asked, surveying the battle around him. The surge of vampires and Fae and werewolves weren't unlike the waves of a bloody ocean. When his eyes lingered on the colossus in the distance, a searing pinpoint of golden light flashed in his vision.

"That's it…" The voice said something more, but it was weak, drowning in something else.

It took him some time to place the voice, weakened as it was, but the vision of Dirge with the necromancer, the forest reborn, and the whispered words of the man as he passed out told Terrence he was probably right. Once more he looked back at the girl and the were-wolves, and then he struck out toward the colossus and the only thing in the world that shone brighter than the sun.

✦　✦　✦

TERRENCE'S MEMORIES OF the past few hours slowly came back to his mind like enough puzzle pieces had been settled that he could see the patterns of the bigger picture. He had been in Greenville with Dirge and the other ghosts. But something had called to him, dragged him into a darkness like nothing he'd ever seen before.

And by the time he'd reappeared, he wasn't himself anymore. But that girl had given him some piece of himself back. And he was fairly certain that what had dragged him through that darkness had been the necromancer, and that somehow the necromancer had summoned the colossus.

But if Damian had summoned this thing, why would he have given it a beacon for Terrence to follow? If he summoned it as a weapon, or transport, or…

But the longer Terrence studied the movements of the colossus, the longer he realized it didn't appear to be on anyone's side. If it was a weapon, it was a weapon with no allegiance, striking down fairies and were-wolves and ghosts without prejudice, or hesitation. At times it appeared to be traveling with the helmeted vampires, the dark-touched he'd heard them called. In time, those too fell prey to the colossus.

But the golden light was the only thing in the world that looked different to his eye. He couldn't fight the compulsion to find out why.

Terrence had learned many things in the skirmish-es he'd witnessed and participated in during the Civil War. There was a part of his brain that marveled at the fact he was still using some of those lessons so long after he'd died. He stayed at the edge of the tree line whenever he could, and when there was no tree line, he knew to hide near the base of the bizarre buildings of the fairies. Impossibly smooth steeples and spires soared toward the heavens where they hadn't been brought down into ruins.

But even there on the outskirts, he didn't go wholly unnoticed. Creatures of blackened bark took notice of him when he moved out of sequence with his fellow ghosts. Dead, milk-white eyes caused his very soul to shiver. When he slowed his pace, and matched his steps to those of the other ghosts plodding along in the colossus's path, the dark creatures would lose their interest and turn their unnerving gaze upon others engaged on the battlefield.

Not all of his enemies were so easily dissuaded. More than one of the armored vampires charged at him, as if they sensed he was different, other, and needed to be removed from this world. But Terrence's journey from Greenville to Falias had had many side effects.

The first of the creatures leaned in as if to sniff at the old soldier, only to have a bayonet rammed through its eye before Terrence pulled the trigger and fired a ghostly lead slug into its braincase. Terrence stared down at the broken heap of flesh, and massive fangs protruding from the shadows of the thing's helmet. Darkness oozed from the thing's lips, as if it had dragged a piece of hell up with it.

Terrence moved deeper into Falias, avoiding what enemies he could, and bringing low those he couldn't. He still didn't understand the mechanics of the gun he carried in his hand. He had no need to reload it, no need for powder, paper, or even fire. It was an impossible thing, but so was the fact he still stood.

After a time, Terrence came to realize he'd crossed the enemy lines. No longer did he see the werewolves or hear the howls and the shriek of claws on metal. Instead, he found the horrible skeletons and their riders posted along various city blocks. They stood still, waiting, but none of them moved against the ghost. Each of them seemed to look away, as if something had told them to ignore him.

The streets of the golden city narrowed the deeper Terrence explored them. The stone beneath his feet that had been little more than rubble not a quarter mile before were now shined like a captain's boot. The very rock glowed with a life of its own, but the looming silhouette of the colossus darkened everything around it.

Most of the skeletons turned away as Terrence grew close to them, but not all of them did. A few reached out for the ghost, only to have their movements turn jerky and unnatural. Terrence almost laughed to himself at the thought of a skeleton's movement being natural. Nothing felt very natural anymore. Except perhaps Dirge, and the tension of guitar strings beneath his fingers.

But those weren't here. In this place, the music was overwhelmed by the screams of the dying and the cacophony of a distant battle. Terrence moved into a dark alley, hidden from the sun, and even from the colossus. But losing sight of his goal, losing sight of that flashing golden beacon, unsettled him to his core.

A heavy sense of worry and dread crawled up into Terrence's throat, until he hurried out the other end of the alley and could once again see the hulking form of the colossus, and the flashing light hidden in the flesh of its back. He was closer now. For whatever reason, the colossus had slowed. It stared down at some unseen point deeper in the city.

Terrence didn't waste the opportunity. He no longer tried to follow the even march of the ghosts he'd left behind. Instead, he hurried, like a child trying to escape the monsters in the shadows.

"Who are you?" A voice boomed from behind and just above Terrence.

He glanced back and frowned at the small fairy hovering above him. In his experience, most of the Fae tended to ignore ghosts. But Terrence supposed things were different now that the ghosts could hurt them.

The fairy casually drew the sword from the sheath on his back, narrowly avoiding his black and white wings as he leveled the whip-thin blade at Terrence.

"You can't kill me," Terrence said. And though his voice sounded sure, for all he knew the Fae could easily strike him down.

"Aye," the fairy said. "I might not be able to kill you, but I can cut little pieces off you. It won't feel so good."

Terrence crossed the block, the smooth marble-like street whispering beneath his translucent footsteps. "You fight for him? Nudd?"

The fairy, now hovering a few feet in front of Terrence, frowned. His wings pulsed slowly as he hung just out of reach of Terrence, but did not impede the ghost's progress in any way.

"You ask dangerous questions, ghost. Why aren't you falling in line like all the others?"

A raven cried out above them, drawing both of their gazes to the sky. The bird circled, the fairy cursed, and Terrence continued on his way.

"You're with the Inn?" the fairy asked.

The Inn? It took a moment for Terrence's memories to coalesce. He'd heard the name, but there was more to it. The words came out of his mouth as a whisper. "The Obsidian Inn."

"Aye," the fairy said. "Do you stand with them?"

Terrence wasn't sure what the right answer was. He couldn't be sure who the fairy was, but no matter which side the Fae stood on, Terrence thought there might be one alliance he'd respect. "I stand with the forest gods, and I live in the woods of the one called Dirge."

The fairy frowned and then smiled. He sheathed his sword. "You're not with Nudd. How did you get so deep into the city? Why aren't you under the control of whatever's drawing all of the dead here?"

Terrence shook his head. "I think I am. I have to get to the necromancer."

"The necromancer?" The fairy asked.

Terrence gestured toward the colossus. "He … saved me. Released me. I think it's why I'm free." Terrence frowned. He wasn't truly free, but his actions were more his own than those of the ghosts he'd seen on the battlefield.

"Damian?" The fairy burst into a string of curses that Terrence was fairly sure were Gaelic.

Terrence turned the question around on the fairy. "Who are you?"

"Name's Angus," he said. "And I'm no friend of Nudd."

"There's a girl with the werewolves," Terrence said. "They need help. Back in the fields, right at the outskirts of the city. I think they're trying to get back to the Obsidian Inn, but there's more in their way than they know."

"Dammit Morrigan," Angus muttered, looking up at the raven that had returned. "Go," he shouted. "I'll learn what I can and meet you at the Inn."

The raven released an unnaturally loud call and rocketed back the way Terrence had come.

"You're in luck, dead man," Angus said. "I know the streets better than most. And you're only a block away from being obliterated by one of the higher orders of dark-touched."

"The vampires?"

Angus nodded. "Follow me. I'll get you as close as I can, but I'm no match for whatever Damian has become." The fairy looked up at the shadow in the distance, and something like grief crossed his face for only a second before steel replaced it. "Let's go."

CHAPTER FOUR

A MILLENNIUM HE'D waited for this. Every year, every day, spent tinkering and nudging and preparing for this fight. And it was bearing more fruit than he ever could have hoped.

A slow smile crawled across Nudd's face in the torchlight, a smile that he tempered when footsteps sounded in the hall. Light danced across stone in the underground hall.

"The titan is nearly here, Nudd," a gravelly voice said from the edge of the darkness of the room. Behind the flickering light, shadows waited, deep enough to make his guards invisible, or hide an assassin.

Nudd turned toward the helmeted form, its eyes lost within. "I told you to call me 'Lord.' Our plan is progressing well enough. Soon the Seal between you and those of your kind trapped in the Burning Lands will fall."

"Many of our lords were stranded in the outer rings." The vampire paused. "We've seen your weapon.

We grow concerned you may turn it against your allies."

Nudd narrowed his eyes and looked away. "Damian will do my bidding. You've also seen the commoners. Your kind will have a feast for ages."

Nudd understood the vampire's loyalty stayed with his master. The dark-touched were ruled over by an entity that any being with common sense would fear, and he'd long suspected the vampires shared a hive mind. And their alliance had not come cheaply. But he had the weapon now, he'd turned Vesik, and the timing for the rest had to be perfect.

Success would mean Nudd could finally return the Courts to their rightful place. There would be no need to hide in Faerie, and magic could flow freely between the realms once more. It would no longer be restrained to the rivers of ley lines, but it could be an ocean once more, limitless, and his people would thrive in a new oasis.

Geb, the old Watcher, had once asked Nudd if he thought the price of the alliance was worth it. If the price of betraying his own wife had been worth it. But Geb didn't understand. Returning Faerie to its rightful status was not a choice. It was this, or the slow inevitable death of the Fae as the magic that sustained them ran too thin in the commoners' realm. Things would be right again one day. He'd make sure of it, by force when necessary, and by sacrifice when there was no other path.

"You've taken the commoners' weapons," the vampire said. "With them, you have no need of us."

Nudd blew out a short breath. "Detonating them would be the end of us. No magic can draw that poison out of the earth once it's unleashed. It would outlive us all."

"That is not a problem for my masters."

It wouldn't be a problem for any of them if they were dead. But Nudd didn't speak those thoughts aloud.

"Still your tongue," Nudd said, his voice growing low and dangerous. For a moment he considered lopping off the head of yet another dark-touched vampire. But a small part of him was concerned one of their masters would descend on the realm if he killed too many, and Nudd was not sure he could defeat one of them without aid. So he let it go, instead allowing the vampire to draw another breath, letting his footsteps soil the golden tiles beneath his feet.

He still owed the dark-touched a favor, and these were not beings to whom one wished to owe favor. But Damian, Damian's powers, those would turn the tide. Nudd would restore the glory of Faerie, and then turn his creature on the lords of the dark-touched themselves. The necromancer would rain down more pain and blood than even Camazotz could imagine.

Nudd's smile widened as the footfalls of a giant reverberated on the earth above him.

CHAPTER FIVE

TERRENCE FOLLOWED ANGUS through the tangled narrow alleys of another street. The fairy zipped forward and checked each intersection before they crossed through sunlight and back into shadow. More of the skeletons waited at every corner, but what unnerved Terrence more were the gargoyle-like vampires perched along the edges of the roof tops. There were more dark-touched here than he'd ever seen before, except perhaps at the fight in Greenville, when this mess started.

"And you're sure that's Damian?" Angus asked.

Terrence grew more vigilant as the shadows deepened around them. "I can't explain it." He tried to keep his voice low, barely above a whisper, but the fairy still seemed to be able to understand him just fine. "The girl, she touched me, and I could see it all again. I could see it all again, the flashback of when I died. But there were other people there this time ... The girl behind us, the necromancer stood above me. It wasn't how I remembered dying. They weren't there."

Angus nodded. "Aye. One of the necromancer's visions. They call them knowings. Happens when he touches the dead. He's close with the girl, with Vicky. It may be her bond is why you saw something out of the normal."

"*Normal*," Terrence said with a small laugh. "As if such a thing exists."

"Oh aye, if you've met Damian and his ragtag bunch of misfits, you get a whole new perspective on normal."

Angus slid his sword into the keyhole on a brick set in a towering wall. He jostled around, cursed, and reached his arm into the space beside his sword. Angus grunted with the effort until the stone turned like a deadbolt. The doorway that had been impossibly flush with the golden stone slid open. "Come on."

Terrence followed Angus into the building, only to have anxiety expand in his chest once he lost sight of the colossus again. It was a terrible feeling, and one he couldn't shake. The sooner they were out of the shadows, the better. At least that had been his initial thought, but as reason returned to his mind, common sense bled through the cracks of dread trying to consume him. It was better for them to be hidden. Perhaps he didn't have the reassurance of being able to see the colossus, but they had the safety in being hidden from the dark-touched.

"We're safe from the vampires here?" Terrence asked.

"Oh yes," Angus said. "This is a place they could never walk. I was a little concerned you might not be able to walk here, given the magicks that protect this place. Have you felt anything odd?"

Terrence shook his head. "Nothing new. A little unease."

Angus gave a sharp nod of approval. "Good. Honestly, you probably would've been dead already if this wasn't going to go right."

"Has anyone ever told you you're not very reassuring?"

"Just my cousin. But she's dead now."

Terrence hesitated. "Did you kill her?"

"Cassie?" Angus gave a quick shake of his head and snorted a wholly inappropriate chuckle.

The sound was loud enough Terrence worried it was dangerous.

"If I didn't know better I'd think Adannaya's humor had worn off on you. No, I didn't kill my cousin. An Old God by the name of Gurges did. He's dead now. He'd been under the command of Hern, held allegiance to Hern, and Hern has done my family

27

much damage. I'm here to kill him."

The realization was like a slap to Terrence. "But Damian..."

"Aye," Angus said. "It put a wee wrinkle in my plan."

"How did you—"

The sword strike came from nowhere. Terrence didn't understand how Angus managed to keep his head, much less avoid the strike altogether.

Massive talons soared out of the shadows of the ceiling, reaching for Terrence's eyes. He barely raised his rifle in time as the enormous owl crashed into him, the talons digging into the translucent wood of his rifle. The owl scratched at Terrence's pale flesh, splitting his skin though no blood oozed from his wounds. The owl cocked its head and then launched itself back into the air.

In that same moment, Angus exploded, the small fairy becoming a burly, musclebound warrior as he faced off with the owl's rider. Terrence leveled his rifle at the other Fae. Golden accents adorned the bright armor and an owl's claw was carved into the forehead of the Fae's helmet. Metal rang against metal as swords collided and sparked in the shadows. Angus forced the fairy backward before landing a quick shot to his knee, causing the other fairy to collapse.

"Leave this place," Angus said. "I have no quarrel with you. I'm here for Hern."

"You trespass upon the new Royal Courts of Faerie. You die."

Terrence swung his rifle around, trying to find a clear shot past Angus's wings.

Angus grimaced, and when the fairy lunged for him, Angus grabbed the sword by the blade, deflecting it just enough that his own sword could ram up through the other fairy's unarmored neck. Blood filled the Fae's mouth before the white eyes went blank and the knight collapsed into a screaming mass. The owl hovered and then rocketed off into the darkness above.

"Hurry," Angus said. "There will be more."

They dodged through the corridors of the place the knight had called the new Royal Courts. Terrence didn't think they could have been *that* new, as Angus knew his way around. He led them from shadow to shadow, light barely touching them at all. Every distant sound that could have been a flap of wings sent Terrence's gaze toward the rafters, compounding the dread in his gut. Only there weren't truly rafters here. There were shadows and towering sculptures of violence and punishment. Brilliant stone carvings of wars long past and glories that were anything but.

What seemed to have taken hours had in reality

only taken them a few minutes as they traversed the halls of that place. Angus made his way to a wall, slid a brick to the side, and opened another hidden doorway into the light.

Terrence frowned, not understanding how their trip through the hall had brought them so much closer to the colossus. But the sight of the thing untied some of the anxiety in his chest, bringing him an odd sort of relief. But whatever relief Terrence felt, Angus's rigid posture told the ghost his companion didn't share it. The Fae stared down at the half-moon auditorium over which the colossus loomed. Inside stood a small cadre of dark-touched vampires, and a horn-helmed figure draped in dark cloth.

"Nudd," Angus growled.

CHAPTER SIX

"I'M AFRAID THIS is going to be up to you," Angus said.

Terrence looked up at the towering form of the fairy beside him. It didn't appear Angus was happy with what he had said. But it also didn't look like Terrence could say anything to change his mind.

"What do I do?" Terrence asked.

One moment Angus towered over the ghost, and the next he had snapped into a much smaller form. He settled onto the arm of a sconce holding a torch and let out a slow breath. "Being this close to Nudd is too big a risk. His people will recognize me. They know I'm allied with the Obsidian Inn."

Terrence studied the colossus. "And what does that matter now? What do you hope to hide from them?"

"As much as I can." Angus looked off into the distance, back the way they'd come, as if he could see through those walls, see the battlefield beyond, and see the allies they'd left behind. The fairy turned back and held Terrence's gaze. "You get to the light you told me about. Find out what the hell it is. If your contact with Vicky somehow broke through to Damian, it could very well be him."

"And what do I do if it is?"

"You run. You get out of there as fast as you can. Find me, or the wolves, or the Morrigan. If there's a chance we can get Damian back, we have to take it."

The determination on Angus's face reminded Terrence of the words the necromancer had spoken in Greenville, and the passion that had helped drive Dirge into a new alliance.

He might not have known the fairy long, but if Angus was anything like his friends, he deserved a little trust.

Of course, trust didn't matter all that much just then. Even if Angus told him to turn back now, Terrence doubted that he could. The pull toward the colossus was undeniable. Irresistible even. He only hoped that compulsion would let him help his friends, and not damn them all. These thoughts he didn't speak aloud, as he didn't know how the fairy might react. But doubt settled in his heart beside the hope. It reminded him of the calm before the battles he'd fought so long ago.

Terrence nodded. "Find the girl, will you?"

"Vicky?"

"Yes, I'm afraid she's in trouble. Save her if you can."

Angus let out a humorless laugh. "I don't know what you'll see out there ..." He gestured to the massive black form. "But there's no shame in running. Survive. Get word back to the Obsidian Inn. I'll do what I can about the girl."

"Thank you."

Angus met Terrence's gaze. The fairy flexed his wings and vanished into the skies.

✦   ✦   ✦

TERRENCE KEPT TO the shadows. He stayed close to the walls when he didn't have the darkness to mask him. Whatever was happening inside the little amphitheater had drawn the attention of every creature in the area. Terrence moved silently beneath the dark-touched vampires perched on the roofs. But the closer he got, the more he saw the shifting shadows in every crevice of the street. The flesh of the dead hid between the golden tiles. The closer he came to the colossus, the more obvious it became, for they were all an extension of his power, his form. And that was a terrible sight to behold.

Much to Terrence's horror, he realized he was

going to have to walk across the bark-like substance. There was no open path leading up to the colossus. The ghost took a deep breath he didn't need and strode forward. The first step felt as if the blackened bark pushed back, and the second crunched beneath his translucent boot. By the third, something changed. The substance forming the back of the colossus's leg parted like flesh around a blade. Terrence hesitated. This felt right. This was what he was supposed to do. He hurried into the small pathway carved in the creature's flesh. It had formed a kind of staircase. It felt solid under his feet, but it trembled and vibrated as the massive figure swayed.

The path behind Terrence collapsed as he moved. There was no turning back now. Whatever that beacon was, he would reach it.

✦   ✦   ✦

VOICES SOUNDED AROUND Terrence. It took him some time to realize they were echoes from whatever was happening in the auditorium below. He could make out a few words at first, but the farther he moved up the colossus, the more the words became no more than a buzz in the background. If he thought the shifting flesh and staircases were odd as he traversed the calf of the colossus, things only got stranger from there. Once he reached the knee of the beast, the flesh no longer shifted beneath him. Instead, it grew out to the side like a branch covered in the rough bark of dead things.

Terrence glanced up, but the way the colossus's leg was bent, he couldn't see the golden beacon anymore. He wished at that time he could fly like the fairies. But the most he'd ever seen a ghost do was hover, and calling attention to himself here could spell his end. Terrence couldn't tell if it had all been an illusion, or if that newly formed branch was the least strange thing he'd see today. Terrence squeezed the nearest of the branches and whispered, "Don't let me fall now."

He wasn't really sure if he could die, or die again, if he fell from this height, but he was fairly certain it wouldn't feel good. He had some sensation back in his hands and arms ever since Damian had instilled him with energy in Greenville. As much as it had been a blessing to be able to feel the strings of his guitar beneath his fingertips once more, he could also feel pain again.

Terrence swung forward on one of the branches of flesh, but nothing happened. He dangled there for a moment, watching with some distress as the stairs he'd been standing on vanished under his boots, but a short time later a branch oozed its way out of the crease of the colossus's knee. Terrence grabbed it and another rose up. He wasn't able to reach this one, but he lodged his feet on the first branch and pulled himself up.

From there, he could make the short hop to grab the next. This pattern continued for a time, and Terrence marveled at the fact that he wasn't short of breath, and that even as his muscles flexed to pull his weight from branch to branch, he didn't feel the exhaustion in his bones. It was a strange thing, as in life he'd never been great at pull ups. He'd had friends that enjoyed climbing rocks, but Terrence would usually have waited for them at the bottom of the mountains, prepping the camp and writing a new song. But here he felt none of it. As he grew more sure of the branches, and the absence of enemies, he hurried up the black-ened flesh as fast as his body would carry him.

He reached the waist of the colossus, now higher than several of the buildings around him, before he saw the faces. They weren't everywhere, but between one step and the next, milky white eyes rose up from the wall of the giant's back. Empty mouths filled with nothing but shadows and whispered groans. He hurried past them, unnerved at the things and the pounding sense of dread inside his chest. Whatever they were, it wasn't something he cared to stay close to. He'd seen them on the battlefield before, shadows and darkness. When he was alive, some men told him tales about the things they'd witnessed crawling through the grass around their fallen brothers. Terrence had never been one for ghost stories, but things had changed.

While he was lost in those thoughts, an arm tore free of the flesh of the colossus. The bark-like appendage wrapped around Terrence as if it were a vise.

Terrence cursed, and then snapped his mouth closed. He'd been lucky enough not to run into any of the dark-touched vampires on the back of this colossus. But if he screamed now, screamed at the pain of claws and fingers digging into his legs, into his gut, they'd be on him in moments. This was nothing like the dull pressure of the owl's talons, this was a piercing fire. Terrence tried to shift the barrel of the gun strapped to his back into the face of the monster, but even if he had managed it, the shot would call attention to him. He felt as if his bones were creaking, as though the pressure of a mountain was bearing down on him. In a desperate effort, he pulled the sword from the scabbard at his hip. It sang out, a deep golden light that slashed through the arm pinning him down. The flesh crumbled away only for the shower of ash to be reabsorbed a few feet below him. But he lost his grip on the branch and he couldn't stifle the scream as the creature released him and he fell forward.

CHAPTER SEVEN

T HE SKY BECAME earth and the earth sky. And then everything went dark. Terrence crashed onto a platform that hadn't been there. The flesh of the colossus had flashed out, catching him and carrying him back to the branches he'd used to climb.

Terrence's breath came hard and fast. It wasn't that he needed the air, but the panic, the certainty something horrible was about to happen when he hit the ground, was a feeling he couldn't escape. The colossus shook, and Terrence glanced down the way he'd come. It wasn't a sight he wanted to see. His scream, or the motion on the back of the giant, had called them. At least two of the dark-touched vampires leapt out and were climbing the colossus far faster than he'd be able to.

But it didn't stop him. He dove for the branches. Three quick steps, a leap, and he was swinging once more. He moved as fast as he could, ignoring the milk-white eyes when they appeared in the walls around him. Terrence climbed faster and faster, his feet slipping, only to be caught by a resurgence of the flesh of the colossus. He reached another platform, above the waistline of the giant, and he dared to glance back. What he saw put his jaw on his chest.

The colossus was having none of the dark-touched. Bodies cloaked in wisps of shadows oozed out of the colossus's flesh only to wrap the dark-touched in a silent embrace. The vampires vanished, reaching out as if for help before they were simply absorbed into the mass of the colossus. None resurfaced. That's what would've happened to Terrence. He knew it. And perhaps if he stayed in one place too long, it would still happen.

His jaw flexed as he ground his teeth together and looked up the back. Something like a ladder of dead flesh replaced the branches. As if silver bones had been inlaid along the spine, and Terrence sprinted up them.

He focused on each handhold. If they'd been evenly spaced, he could've fallen into a rhythm, but some were set at odd angles. Others were slick, as though coated in blood and oil. So instead, he focused on his grip, focused on one boot rising up a rung and settling in place before he leapt up another. His pace was good, but he'd seen how fast the vampires could move. And fairies could fly, which meant if the wrong person noticed him, or the wrong creature, he didn't have a chance.

It wasn't until the rungs disappeared that Terrence risked another glance back. He was high now. Too high. He'd never had a fear of heights, but the vision below unnerved him. It was like a leaning off the side of an enormous building, with nothing but air and pavement between you and death.

But the vampires were nowhere to be seen. If the first group that had given pursuit were the alarm, the colossus had made short work of them, silencing whatever klaxon they'd hope to raise by smothering it. With the rungs of the makeshift ladder gone, Terrence continued up, using breaks in the colossus's flesh to leverage himself higher.

He kicked at it with his boot, and split the charred flesh wide to get a good foothold where he could. Terrence hadn't seen many of the Fae as he rose higher on the back of the colossus. Just over the hunch of the creature's back, Terrence could see the golden beacon once more. A few more steps, and the flesh of the giant flattened out, giving him a place to rest. Though his body didn't need it, his mind greatly appreciated it.

The call of the beacon had done nothing but grow stronger as Terrence neared, like a cable tied to his heart that drew more taut with every step. The golden light was nearly blinding now, and it made Terrence fairly certain he was the only one who could see it. If the creatures below or around the buildings had been aware of it, he had little doubt he wouldn't have been left so alone to climb the colossus.

But now he was there. He frowned at the small gap in the charred and blackened flesh. He knelt and pried a section of it away, only to realize that what waited inside was the bare flesh of a man's neck. He reached out to touch that pale golden patch. The world flashed brilliant white around him; it wasn't the blinding vision that he experienced when the girl, Vicky, had touched him. This was different. This felt like coming home.

The voice was weak, but it was there. And he knew it.

"Take the pack. Take the pack to Vicky."

It was Damian's voice. Terrence tried to dig the necromancer out of the colossus. But with every fistful of flesh he tore away, it filled with the charred covering of the monster.

"Not monster," Damian's voice whispered. "Gravemakers. Get the bag to Vicky. The innkeeper. Go."

Terrence cursed in frustration. Every bit of flesh that he could tear away from the colossus reformed in an instant. He unsheathed the sword at his waist when he found the strap. The gravemakers frantically tried to close around his hand, but he would not relent. Terrence felt the leather stretch out when the colossus tried to pull Damian back in earnest, and the entire beast moved, shaking Terrence's foothold.

But his sword slid in easily. The first strap severed, and he leaned in, fishing for the second he knew must be there. But his sword missed, and it caught the flesh of the necromancer instead. This time, soaked in Damian's blood, the flash came to him like a thunder-clap.

His life replayed as if in slow motion until it came screaming back to his death, back to Dirge, and those the last moments, his resurrection at the hands of the necromancer, and his awakening at the hands of the child. The child, Vicky. Terrence screamed as he leaned into the colossus and ripped his sword back out through the charred flesh. The second strap separated and the bag ripped away. Again he reached for the necromancer, but Damian was gone.

The blinding light of the beacon faded as Damian disappeared. The platform trembled beneath Terrence as if whatever control Damian had over the flesh of the colossus was waning. It tilted until there was no place for him to grab hold. He cursed as he started to slide downward, barely managing to find a handhold and save himself from a plummet of God knows how far. But with the straps cut on the backpack, Terrence had trouble balancing it. He held on to a small hook at the top, but it was interfering with his grip, making movement down the colossus much harder.

He was going to be seen. He was going to be caught. And he didn't know why, but in his heart he knew if he failed here, they were all doomed.

CHAPTER EIGHT

VICKY WOKE WITH a scream. Wherever she was, it was dark. And she wasn't alone. She'd been in dark places before, disoriented, and torn to pieces.

She'd learned much.

A soulsword exploded in her hand, and Vicky barely caught the flap of wings as a fairy rocketed away from her.

"Easy lass!"

"It's okay, little one," Wahya said, shuffling around the fairy and crouching down beside her. "You're safe."

Vicky's heart pounded in her chest. She trusted Wahya. He was one of the few that she trusted with her life. But the fairy … she wasn't so sure.

Wahya caught her staring, and glanced back at Angus. "He's a friend. He's practically family to Aideen and Foster. Cousin of Cara."

Vicky let the soulsword recede until it snapped out of existence. Angus summoned a small light that showed more of the room. She could make out golden stone surrounding them, but it was faded, as if its very life force had been drained away long ago. That's how she almost always thought of them when she saw the stones of Falias. That golden glow was like the rock had a life of its own.

Her thoughts scattered when she remembered the vision. "Terrence. We have to get to Terrence."

"He's chasing Damian," Angus said.

Vicky pressed her palm to her forehead. "He has a … he has the backpack. He…" She squeezed the bridge of her nose, a dagger of pain threatening to make her sick. "We need it."

"You need rest," Wahya said. "We can go later."

Vicky shook her head. The pain began to recede, ever so slightly, and she drew herself up to her feet. "We have to go."

"Damian's in the heart of Falias," Angus said, exchanging a look with Wahya. "It's not safe passage."

"Not much is," Wahya said. "A small force would be better."

"No," Vicky said, the harshness of the word bringing silence around her. "I'm not risking any of you. Stay here. I'm taking Jasper."

A small ball of fluff trilled in the corner. The fact Vicky hadn't realized he was there made her question the acuity of her perceptions. But the vision had been powerful, and the strength behind it was overwhelming. Damian was still alive.

Vicky paused beside Jasper. "Did you get Enda and her family out?" She glanced over her shoulder at the werewolf and the fairy. Pale light glinted in Wahya's sunburst eyes.

"They're safe, little one. Deep inside the Inn behind the guard of a forest god, so I am told."

"Good. Then … then Jonathan and Hess didn't die for nothing."

Wahya and Angus watched her go as she started up the stairs that led to an ancient carved door. When Vicky pushed through it, daylight threatened to blind her. But the oddest thing happened. When she looked back at the door she'd just passed through, it wasn't there. Whatever spells were worked upon that building, they were damned powerful. Vicky suspected Morrigan had something to do with it, although it could have been Ward. Whatever the case, she could worry about it later. She had bigger priorities.

"Let's go," she said to Jasper, and the dragon didn't miss his cue. The furball exploded into the massive scaly form of the winged beast.

✦ ✦ ✦

ANGER BOILED IN Vicky's gut as she clung to the spines

on Jasper's back and they climbed higher into the sky. She knew where they were now. She knew all about the basilisk skeleton below them in the courtyards not far from the entrance to the Obsidian Inn. They were in the outskirts, the slums, where the Fae either hadn't rebuilt, or had fought so regularly that even the most gifted of their engineers couldn't rebuild before the city would fall again. But that wasn't what angered her. What irritated her now was the fact she was so far back. She'd been on the front lines, so close to Damian she could practically reach him.

Jasper growled beneath her, and Vicky patted the great beast's neck. He had grown more adept at detecting her moods, and she was grateful for it. More than once he'd pulled her back from the edge of rage or despair. Her time with Drake had helped calm her somewhat, but the world still enraged her at times, and that could be a deadly thing. She had access to powers that helped bring the Destroyer low, slayed demons, and cut the flesh of monsters not of this world. Losing control put everyone she loved at risk. The danger her friends were in infuriated her, but now maybe there was some faint hope, some wild spark, Damian was still in there.

Vicky clenched her jaw and leaned in closer to Jasper's scales. He'd taken them higher than she expected, but it was a smart approach. They were high enough now they weren't going to encounter anything short of an owl knight. And an owl knight didn't stand a chance against a girl and her dragon.

Shortly after the thought crossed her mind, a winged form glided past far below them. On the broken ground beneath the owl knight, she could see the crater where Damian had surfaced in Falias, not far from the platform where they'd rescued Liam, Lachlan, and Enda. Soon they were gliding over the battlefield where she'd touched the ghost, and as her eyes trailed toward the horizon, the massive form of the colossus was unmistakable.

It was still Damian, of that she was sure. But it was something else too. Something darker, and she didn't think it was just Hern. Hern was certainly part of whatever that creature was now, but the sheer weight of the gravemakers and the souls tied up inside of that thing was like a black hole, bending the nearby ley lines to its will.

Another of the owl knights crossed her line of sight, and Jasper rose higher, cutting into the edge of a cloud bank. Vicky shivered at the damp cold. She'd be grateful when they were on the ground again. A storm was moving in, and it would soak the land as surely as the blood of the coming war.

Jasper didn't reach the clouds fast enough. She saw the sharp bank of one of the owl knights. She had a split second to decide to chase the knight, or vanish into the clouds and hope the knight thought it was a trick of the light. But Vicky knew the Fae better than that, knew their cunning, and understood how well they could perceive the world around them.

"Get them," Vicky snapped.

She didn't need to say anything more. She didn't need to guide the dragon. Jasper had seen the knights too, following them with his giant black eyes. But now they were locked on like a hawk with a mouse beneath its talons.

They skirted the cloud bank before Vicky flattened herself against the dragon, rising and falling with the heaving of his wings as Jasper increased their speed into a suicidal descent. The cold wind bit at Vicky's cheeks. She squinted against the breeze, the air like the edge of a blade. The first drops of precipitation crashed against her forehead a moment before a surprised-looking owl knight crashed against the jaws of the dragon. Jasper crunched twice and belched out a blue fireball. If the bird or its rider had survived the initial impact, there would be nothing left after that hellish blue flame. Vicky caught the spiraling pile of ash out of the corner of her eye as Jasper turned and rocketed toward Damian.

Things below them started to move.

"They've seen us," Vicky said. She'd hoped they'd been fast enough, but either the knight had already issued a warning, or another of Nudd's soldiers had seen them. "Hurry. We need to get to Damian *now*."

Jasper stretched his neck out until he was a streamlined as possible. Each flap of his wings was nearly perpendicular to his body, and the sensation was something like being shot out of a high-speed roller coaster. Only it didn't stop; it just increased in speed until the colossus that seemed so far away was suddenly in front of them.

The soulswords weren't the only one of Damian's abilities Vicky had inherited. In some ways, they may have been the most useful, but currently Vicky was far more thankful of her ability to see ghosts. A small army of them marched toward the colossus, penetrating the walls and alleys and byways of Falias, all except for one. One lone ghost clung to the back of the colossus, the bark-like flesh trying to draw it in.

Vicky caught a flash like steel, flickering around the ghost, as Jasper spread his wings and slowed before they crashed into Damian's back. They were close enough now Vicky could see it was Terrence. And in the ghost's hand was Damian's backpack. The backpack where he kept everything he thought he needed for a battle. And that's what she had to get to the innkeeper.

But how in the hell had Terrence gotten it? How could he have climbed onto Damian's back? Was Damian able to help him? A million questions raced through Vicky's mind. But those could wait. That vision had been a message, and for now she knew what they needed. Jasper dropped and let his claws dig into the colossus's back.

The entire mass of gravemaker flesh shifted, and Vicky watched in horror as a blackened bark-like arm stretched toward them. The thing was as tall as a skyscraper, with a hand large enough to crush Aeros in a single blow.

"Come on!" Vicky shouted to Terrence, worried the ghost might not hear her over the distance.

The ghost looked up, wide-eyed. "Hell yes, girl." Terrence turned his rifle on the gravemaker crawling out of the flesh beside him and fired.

The face disintegrated, but the thunder of the gun-shot drew the attention of everything around them. And even if it hadn't, the sudden roar of the giant, the earth-shaking bellow vibrating the earth, would have told the whole damn state something was there.

"Lower," Vicky shouted to Jasper, jerking on one of

his spines.

The gravemakers forming the flesh of the colossus surged at the dragon, grabbing his claws and reaching for his wings. But Jasper was too strong for the individual hands of the gravemakers. They broke away, only to fall and be reabsorbed farther down the colossus. Jasper worked like that for a few seconds, tearing and rending and breaking free until they were finally close enough to Terrence for him to grab hold of Vicky's hand.

Vicky swung him up onto the dragon's back, and with one mighty flame, Jasper burned away the flurry of gravemaker arms reaching out for them. Vicky almost retched as some of the milk-white eyes burst from the intense heat, sending a cascade of viscera and gore down the back of the colossus.

The thing started to turn in earnest. But it wasn't a thing, it was Damian, and far below them stood Nudd, a shadowed form bearing horns.

"Go now!" Vicky screamed.

Her heart tried to hammer through her rib cage as she realized they were in the core of the enemy's forces. If Nudd was here, his most powerful allies would be here. He wouldn't leave himself unprotected. He was too smart for that. But of course he hadn't left himself unprotected. Damian was here. Damian, who had threatened Nudd for so many years, who had perhaps been his biggest threat, now stood calmly by the murdering bastard's side. Well, calmly until Jasper set him on fire.

The thought filled Vicky with a rage that almost matched her fear she wouldn't get her chance to try to reach him. Terrence unleashed a string of curses behind her and buried his head next to the spines on Jasper's back as the dragon surged away from the colossus. The massive arm of the giant just missed the end of the dragon's tail.

But it wasn't only the colossus they were running from now. More owl knights closed on them, and skeletons riding winged things came from the shadows of a dark cloak billowing out from Damian's form.

Vicky looked back at the mass of blackened shadows surging along the ground behind them. Even if they couldn't get to her, get to them, they could follow the dragon back to the Obsidian Inn. They couldn't go there, they'd lead them straight to their allies' stronghold.

"Shit."

CHAPTER NINE

"WHERE THE HELL do we go now?" Vicky shouted into the wind, eyeing the city below her, and hoping a solution to their predicament would reveal itself.

"Take us back to the Inn!" Terrence shouted back.

Vicky shook her head. Going back there now would lead their enemy straight to the Obsidian Inn. "I can't do that."

She glanced back at the ghost, and followed his line of sight toward Damian.

"He's not chasing us …"

"I think some part of him is fighting it," Terrence said. "Whatever's happened to him, there's still some part of him inside that thing."

Vicky looked down at the black sack Terrence hung over one of Jasper's spikes. "What the hell do you have his backpack for?" She turned to the horizon in front of them.

"It's for you. You're supposed to take it to the innkeeper."

Vicky frowned. That wasn't something Terrence would know about, unless Dirge had told him about the innkeeper. But even then, why would Dirge think Damian's backpack should make it back to the innkeeper?

Damian was still in there, and while the fact she was still alive hadn't been enough to calm the fear in her chest, this told her perhaps more of him was left than she thought. More than just the magicks that kept her and Sam alive.

"Can this thing go any faster?" Terrence said, his voice panicked.

Jasper tilted his head back and chuffed. Smoke curled out from the sides of the dragon's jaws.

Vicky had a sarcastic barb ready on the tip of her tongue, but as she turned to shout at Terrence, the words died on her lips. They weren't alone in the skies anymore. The winged army of Gwynn Ap Nudd was in quick pursuit.

"Jasper," Vicky started.

The dragon tilted his head back, and Vicky could've sworn she saw the massive black orbs dilate when he saw what was chasing them. Owl knights were the least of their problems. Out in front of the dark cloud of Nudd's forces flew two dragons. One of them was clearly bigger than Jasper, with great horns lining the beast's neck, and a silver knight perched on its back. But it wasn't just a single fairy knight. As she looked closer, she could see there were two riders on the back of the beast, one garbed in silver armor, and the other in obsidian black. Even as she watched, the looming shadows of the dragons grew. It wasn't that the beasts themselves were increasing in size. No, they were closing the distance more rapidly than Vicky had feared.

She cursed again and leaned against Jasper. "As fast as you can!"

Instead of a sudden increase in the speed of his wing motions, Jasper folded into what amounted to a torpedo, and fell. The force of the wind threatened to peel Vicky's fingers from his spines. She hugged the dragon as best she could. It was difficult, as it was, to hold on in the battering breeze, and it was about to get a hell of a lot bumpier. She watched the buildings rush up around them, until she could almost make out the details of the stone street beneath them before Jasper's wings unfurled and the snap of air against his sinewy flesh was like a gunshot as it pulled taut. A mighty heave threw them forward into an alley barely wide enough for the beast. Scales scraped stone, and Jasper growled as something smashed into the wall above them.

Vicky glanced back in time to see what looked like a bolt of green lightning carving its way through the alley. She could follow the beam back to the dragon above them with the two riders, until the other dragon skipped out of Vicky's line of sight.

Jasper hurtled out of the end of the alley, crouched, then launched himself back into the air. While Vicky's main thought had been to escape the other dragons, she knew Jasper had seen far more battles than her. He'd probably faced many dragons before, far more than just Drake's dragon. Instead of running, he moved to flank them.

The riders hadn't expected it. One moment Jasper had been on the ground, and the next he was above them, his neck curling back, his jaw unhinging, and a hellish fireball tearing down the side of their mount. The knight in black squealed as the fires hit them. Vicky didn't take satisfaction in seeing the rider suffer. He flailed and tried to scrape the fires away, finally summoning a magick to dispel the flames. But it was far too late. He slumped over in the saddle, leaving only the silver rider.

But losing a rider didn't stall the dragon. It twisted about and unleashed a fireball of its own. Jasper pulled back and absorbed the brunt of it on the scales of his belly. But even from her perch between Jasper's spikes, Vicky could feel the heat. Terrence shouted in pain as if the flames had burned the ghost. Jasper whined, a sound Vicky had never heard come from the dragon, and it took a second for her to register the fact that he'd been hurt.

"Get us out here," Vicky said. "As far as you can, underground if we have to."

Jasper moved, but he felt slow, and the other dragon wheeled around, closing for the kill.

The boom of a gunshot echoed behind Vicky. She glanced back to see Terrence with his rifle leveled at the dragon. Small explosions of electric blue burst along the dragon where the bullet struck. She didn't know what he was firing out of that thing, but it didn't seem to be hurting the beast.

The dragon paused to inspect its scales where it had been hit. The delay only lasted a moment, but a moment was all the second dragon needed to come crashing out of the cloud bank above. Despair and betrayal like Vicky had not felt in years washed over her when she saw the claws of Drake's dragon extended toward her, jaws opening as Drake held his sword out to them from atop his mount.

But that despair turned to something else as the head of Drake's mount snapped to the side and a torrent of fire bathed the horned dragon in superheated flame. The second rider didn't have enough time to scream before Drake wheeled his dragon around and snatched the saddle from the back of the horned beast.

"Get out of here, kid!" Drake shouted. "You don't have a chance."

"Why are you with them?" Vicky shouted back.

Drake didn't smile, didn't so much as raise an eyebrow. "Never show your hand."

"Go!" Terrence yelled.

Vicky hesitated and watched the horned dragon spiral out of the air. But the beast shook itself, the wind catching beneath its wings before it hit the earth, propelling its massive form back toward Drake.

She maneuvered Jasper and they soared right over Drake's head. She wasn't sure if she'd regret it, but she said one word. "Innkeeper."

CHAPTER TEN

THEY WERE NEARLY out of the city when Vicky saw the figures. She glanced back at the distant shadows embroiled in flame. Drake could stop their pursuit, but Vicky didn't know if he could survive it. It was mad, to stand alone against those forces. For a time, she came close to turning around, worried about Drake and his insane intervention. But he'd told her to go. He knew how to handle himself.

She turned back to the figures below them and patted Jasper on the neck, indicating a small field where two furry forms had barreled through the city and flagged them down.

As soon as the dragon landed, Jasper snapped back into his furball form. Vicky and Terrence fell several feet, but Vicky had been expecting it. Terrence landed flat on his face with a grunt, cursing at volume.

"Shh," Vicky whispered, choking back a small laugh as the ghost rubbed at his face.

Caroline paced back and forth in her bulky wolf

form. When they ran on all fours, they could almost be mistaken for a wolf. But the effect was startling when the werewolves strode around on their rear legs. Vicky could clearly see how much thicker their hind legs were than their long muscled arms.

"Was that Drake?" Caroline's voice held a more wolfish growl than normal. "I feared we couldn't trust him."

Vicky grimaced and looked back the way they'd come. They were out of sight here, and nothing would catch them for a time.

"We wouldn't have gotten away without him," Vicky said. "I still… I still trust him." Drake had been there for her more than once. Even though she'd stuck her neck out for Drake and his dragon, perhaps no more so than when she flew Jasper through the Arch, hadn't he done the same for her? Especially now. He'd told her stories of that dragon. The horned devil of Gorias, they called it. And it was an apt name.

"You need to go," Terrence said.

Wahya's eyebrows rose slightly as he eyed the ghost. "And what hurry is there?"

Terrence frowned at the werewolf. A small crease formed in his brow and he looked like he was struggling not to talk.

"He has that effect on people," Vicky said. "You

can trust him."

"Vicky needs to get to the innkeeper." Terrence held up the backpack, and Vicky took it from him.

"Rivercene?" Wahya said, making no effort to hide the surprise on his face. The wolf dragged a claw carefully through the fur on his chin. It was an odd gesture on the half-man half-beast, but somehow it fit the stoic old wolf.

"Damian's still in there," Vicky said, her jaw set. "He asked us to do this. It has to be important."

Caroline flexed her claws. "It's worth a shot. The necromancer's stubborn, if nothing else. If they're off at Rivercene, we can help the Obsidian Inn clean up here, and then get back to Antietam."

Wahya's thoughtful expression fell, and a darkness rolled over the sunburst eyes of the golden werewolf.

"You can see him?" Vicky asked with a glance at Terrence. "I mean you can even understand him?"

Wahya gave her a patient smile. "There is much left of the bonds Carter forged with Hugh. And you were tied to Carter, were you not? And Carter was loyal to Hugh. Those lines of power will not crumble so easily. The death of one wolf does not spell the end of a pack."

Caroline released a chuckle that was more like a stuttering wolf's howl. "Take your friend with you," she said, turning to Vicky. "If your ghost is tied to Damian too, it may be good for him to meet Stump and some of the other green men."

Vicky ran her fingers over the severed straps of the backpack. "He's friends with Dirge."

"The forest god Morrigan spoke of," Wahya said, exchanging a glance with Caroline. "That is most interesting. That is a tale I would like to hear in great detail one day."

"Another time, Wahya." Caroline rubbed her clawed paws together, focusing on Vicky. "How long will it take for you to fly to Rivercene?"

Vicky frowned. Jasper was fast, but it was going to take a damn long time. Time she wasn't sure they had. Time she wasn't sure Damian had. She shook her head. "Too long."

"I believe there is a faster way," Wahya said. "Have you not walked through the Abyss before, child?"

Vicky's gaze shot down to the backpack in her hand. She knew what waited inside. The severed hand of a Titan, of Gaia. "She could kill us."

"Perhaps," Wahya said, hunching down until he was eye to eye with Vicky. He gave her a kind smile, still somewhat intimidating with the rather sharp teeth. "But I know what Damian shares with you, I know the bond that keeps you alive, that cut you from the Destroyer. The soul he shares with you and Samantha."

"What?" Caroline asked.

"Guess that cat is out of the bag." Vicky muttered.

"He tied his soul to them?" Caroline asked, her voice caught somewhere between awe and disgust.

"If the worst happens," Wahya said, "Damian will be defeated. And Nudd will have lost his weapon."

Vicky grimaced and scratched Jasper between the eyes. The dragon purred, a high sad trill echoing out from the furball. What Wahya said was true, and perhaps he'd meant it as a poor joke, but he was dead right.

"I'll walk with Gaia."

✦   ✦   ✦

"THAT IS DISGUSTING," Terrence said, staring down at the severed hand Vicky held.

"You … be careful," Caroline said. She gave Terrence, who now looked even paler than before, an awkward grin.

"If you hear word of the River Pack, let me know," Wahya said. "We've had some contact, but I still worry about Hugh and the others."

"I will," Vicky said. She took a deep breath and adjusted the backpack cradled in her arms. Jasper camped out on her shoulder and stayed curled up close to her neck.

Terrence started to say something and then hesitated. "Did you … did you feel it?"

"Feel what?" Vicky asked as she waved to Caroline and Wahya as the werewolves vanished back into the woods.

"I don't know how to explain it. But Damian didn't feel the same. It's like he knew something."

Vicky knew what Terrence meant. Even in the darkest times, Damian seemed to be a light, a beacon to unite his friends. But something was off.

"It's like he knew he was losing," Terrence said.

Vicky grimaced. "Like he knew he was losing control to Nudd."

Terrence took a deep breath and looked off toward the woods. "You really think this is going to kill us?"

"Look on the bright side. You're already dead."

Terrence smiled down at her. "You're okay, kid."

"Put your arm around me and don't let go," Vicky said. "No matter what."

She braced herself as Terrence reached out to her, worried there might be another vision, another knowing. But there wasn't. She was relieved, but then she wondered if it was because Damian was losing himself further. If his powers were being cut off more and more from her and others that he'd touched, that worried her. She ground her teeth together and laced her fingers into the hand of Gaia. She could worry later if she wasn't dead.

The cold flesh closed around her hand, and the light left the world.

CHAPTER ELEVEN

DARKNESS ENVELOPED THEM, and Vicky wondered how stupid of a decision she'd just made. She'd met Gaia before, walked with Damian, and no harm had come to her. But at that time he'd still held the hand of Gaia. He was the rightful heir to the mantle of Anubis. A seventh son, and heir to a power she would never have.

But even as those questions roared through her mind, stars appeared in the distance. A dim golden glow formed beneath her feet, and motes of brilliant yellow light drifted down to the stump of the hand she held. Vicky waited in silence, watching as Gaia's body took shape, until finally the serene face of the Titan came into focus.

"You are not Damian Vesik, and yet..." Gaia frowned. "And yet there is much of his power about you."

"We met before," Vicky said, feeling Terrence's grip tighten around her shoulders as if she were the last shred of sanity in a mad world.

"I remember," Gaia said. "I can only obey the orders of those to whom I am bound."

"Damian would like us to have safe passage to Rivercene," Vicky said, willing to try anything at this point to get out alive.

"I am afraid words are not how this works. Ask me where you wish to go, and we shall see if the compulsion acquiesces." After a brief pause, Gaia added, "Or if you must find other means."

Even as the Titan said, "other means," a tentacle resolved itself just off the edge of the path. And beside it another and another, until their entire right side was flanked by a towering, writhing wall. It moved in slow motion, but that made it no less unnerving.

Terrence cursed, but he fell silent shortly after when Gaia looked upon him.

"Take us to Rivercene," Vicky said, the words coming out rushed, like she just wanted it to be over. And in some ways, the waiting was far worse than anything else.

Gaia tilted her head to the side and a slow smile crawled across her face. "I shall do as you ask."

Vicky blew out a breath. "Fucking hell. At least something went right."

"Such coarse language is not becoming."

"Are you serious?" Vicky asked, blinking rapidly. "Have you met Damian? I mean, have you seriously listened to that man talk?"

Gaia smiled. "Nonetheless, that is no excuse for you to be so crude."

Vicky stared slack-jawed at the goddess, and said no more.

"Damian has been injured," Gaia said after studying Vicky's face for a time. "Has he been lost?"

"If he was lost, I'd be dead," Vicky said. "So I guess that's a pretty good gauge."

Gaia inclined her head. "That must be why responding to your orders is bringing much of the same enjoyment as helping Damian. Some part of him is inside you."

"I think we established that after our little adventure in the Burning Lands."

"Of course, but it is good to know that you may call on me. I will be here should you need assistance. I fear our time together has come to an end for now. Rivercene awaits you. You need only release my hand."

"Thank you," Vicky said. She glanced back at Terrence. "Hold on. If you don't like roller coasters, you're probably not going to enjoy this."

"What's the—"

But Terrence didn't get to finish his question.

Vicky released Gaia's hand, and they fell.

✦　　✦　　✦

VICKY HAD WALKED out of the Abyss before. She knew what to expect as the stars vanished from her vision and the stomach-churning sensation of falling at an impossible speed overcame her. She thought she should have warned Terrence a bit more thoroughly. Almost as fast as the thought had come, light returned, and the evening blossomed before them.

The horizon was a brilliant red and purple, giving the Old Mansion an enduring, if haunted, look. The nearby trees stood as shadowy sentinels, and Vicky would have called it serene if it wasn't for the shouted curses from the ghost wrapped around her.

They crashed into a shallow river a second later. Darkness enveloped Vicky once more as she closed her eyes against the current. She hadn't learned how to swim before she died. Her mother had taught her how to float a bit, so she wouldn't be at a high risk of drowning. It had been the Ghost Pack that taught her to swim, but that had been in the Burning Lands where water didn't behave exactly like water in the common-ers' plane.

Here, each stroke felt like she was pulling against a massive force. As if the water itself resisted her, wanted to hold onto her and keep her in its depths forever.

Vicky's head broke the surface and she squawked. Something had grabbed her back, and just before she lit a soulsword to run it through, she recognized the face of the green man who had lifted her from the water.

"Stump," Vicky said, awkwardly brushing a clump of fiery hair away from her face while she dangled from his hand.

"You appear to be damp," Stump said. "That is not a healthy state for your kind."

Vicky caught sight of Terrence standing beside Stump. He held the backpack, and Jasper shook himself dry before weaving in and out from between Terrence's legs. Vicky had a brief moment of panic as she looked down at her hands. Had she dropped the hand of Gaia? But no, it was still there though she hadn't remembered holding onto it. That explained why swimming through the current had been so hard.

"You've been in the goddess's presence," Stump said. "It is a place of high honor. A place I one time hope to stand as well. Her magicks can have an odd effect on commoners."

Vicky shook her head out as Stump set her down. "I'm not exactly a commoner."

"I suppose you are correct in that," Stump said.

"Perhaps it would be more accurate to say her magicks have a strange effects on humans. For example, I don't know if you've ever seen Damian traverse the Abyss. But every time he exits, he screams like a newborn babe, or as some of the locals like to say, a stuck pig. It's quite piercing, one might even say disturbing. I was not aware such a high-pitched sound could emanate from a fully grown man."

Vicky let out a slow laugh. Once they finally got Damian out of this mess, she had something new to tease him about. Even as her mind tried to say *if* they got him out of this, she choked it back. They'd win or they'd die. There was nothing in between.

Terrence looked the green man up and down. "You're like Dirge."

"There are a great many differences between me and Dirge," Stump said. "I would never deign to compare myself to the forest gods. It is, as the commoners say, like comparing cats to oranges."

A look of utter confusion crossed Terrence's face. He stared at Vicky, as if begging for an explanation. Instead, she just gave him a grin.

"Come now," Stump said. "Friends of Dirge are welcome here. Let us get you inside so you can dry off and get warm. The innkeeper has been expecting you. Though I don't think she's very happy about the fact you walked through the Abyss without Damian. It was risky. And though she may say it was even stupid, I understand the need to hurry."

Even as Stump said the word "hurry," he took slow steps toward the mansion. Vicky followed patiently in his wake, although perhaps patiently wasn't the right word. The thought of getting chewed out by the innkeeper was not a pleasant one.

Vicky eyed Terrence. The ghost didn't have a speck of water on him other than the waterlogged backpack. "I guess you can't get wet. You can still hold the backpack though, which is interesting."

"Oh, I got wet," Terrence said. "I'm just glad the water was fairly warm."

"You're bone dry," Vicky said.

Terrence looked down at his uniform. "It dries off instantly. I can't explain it. I can feel the water, the moisture. Or least I've been able to since Damian changed me. But it doesn't stay."

"It is a memory," Stump said. "It is why you thought the water was warm, and Vicky is shaking from the cold. I suspect your last memory of water was one of a warm river. Things like that linger, never truly leave. It is an impression that will survive far beyond death."

As if it had been his cue, or his reminder Vicky

could get cold, Jasper rolled up to her feet, quickly
climbed her side, and nestled his warm fur against her
neck. Vicky believed Stump's words. How else could
you explain the visceral knowings when she touched a
ghost? Damian experienced much the same, and from
what she'd learned, most necromancers did.

They passed the embankments and a dip beyond it.
Vicky knew this was where the river had once run, so
close to the front of the mansion. The captain who
built the place had been smarter than most. He
researched the floodplain, and he knew what the
highest mark was for any flood in history. So in the end
he showed up all the doubters, and his home did not
flood in his lifetime.

She remembered the story Damian had told her
once about a terrible flood that happened in the 90s.
That had been enough to reach the Old Mansion, but it
had stood for over a hundred years without being
touched by the water. It was only when the commoners
moved the river that the home was at risk. The fact it
was still around, still thriving, said a lot for the bones of
the old place.

Vicky ran her hand along the iron horse head that
sat atop a waist-high pole as they reached the driveway
to the mansion. It was a beautiful place. Three stories, a
turret on the right side of the house, and a steep roof

that loomed over the windows and tiles. Stump stepped cautiously around the concrete of the sidewalk. He took such care around the house that it made Vicky smile.

She led Terrence up the three steps to the front door and looked at the doorframe. It didn't seem all that interesting to her, carved like a braided rope, but she remembered Damian liked it. Vicky reached out to the old metal, a distant sadness settling in her chest, and twisted. As fast as she moved, the bell echoed inside the hall.

"Doesn't anyone just knock anymore?" the inn-keeper's gruff voice said from inside. Her footsteps fell heavy on the hardwood, and it was only a few seconds before the deadbolt snapped in the door and the old wood swung inward.

The innkeeper eyed the trio. She gave a nod to Jasper and a frown to Terrence, but her eyes lingered on Vicky. There was kindness there, a sympathy, and Vicky didn't want it.

That sort of kindness was a weakness, a blade to her armor that cut where she thought she'd guarded her heart closest. And even as Stump nudged her forward, Vicky couldn't stop the tears that spilled over from her eyes.

"Come in," the innkeeper said. "We'll get you a hot

drink and set you by the fire."

"They fell into the river," Stump said. "The ghost dried off, but Vicky did not."

The innkeeper gave Stump a flat look and then ushered the three inside. Once she closed the door behind them, she said, "One day I'm going to turn him into kindling."

CHAPTER TWELVE

VICKY TOOK THE backpack from Terrence and followed the innkeeper as she led them down the hall. It wasn't the first time she'd been to Rivercene. She'd been there enough, and explored it enough, to imagine she'd found every nook and cranny on the three floors of the old home.

"Let's get you a hot chocolate," the innkeeper said.

Vicky almost grumbled about the fact that she wasn't a kid anymore, but if she was being honest, a mug of hot cocoa sounded amazing. Maybe it would help warm her fingertips where the cold dampness of the backpack was already digging in.

She studied one of the old couches in the hallway as they walked by, made of wood and upholstery and far more ornate than any furniture her parents owned. Although if they did own something like that, Vicky imagined her mother would put a "Do not sit here" sign on it like it was in a museum. The thought made her smile.

They passed the grand staircase. Beneath it sat an old upright piano. Vicky slid the hand of Gaia into the backpack as she remembered the story of the other piano in the house, the one Mike had made a ward-stone for—something to protect the inhabitants of the house, both living and dead.

She eyed the display case at the end of the hall. It was full of all sorts of old artifacts and photo albums, but the warmth of the kitchen drew her forward.

Inside waited a peculiar fireplace. More than once she'd seen the kitchen with the hardwood laid all the way to the back until it was flush with the rear of the fireplace. But other times she came in and saw the fire roaring beneath the massive mantle. And instead of wood in the hearth, pitch-black stone caught the ash and flame.

The innkeeper wasn't much taller than the mantle and the long hooks that swung in and out of the fireplace were at chest level for her. She pulled a kettle out of the flames as it rocked forward, and lifted it up with a potholder. Two mugs waited on the counter and Vicky could already smell the chocolate inside.

The milk splashed out of the kettle, and Vicky felt like she was home. She could imagine her own mother dropping marshmallows into the mugs she liked to carry around.

"Take a seat, take a seat," the innkeeper said.

Vicky didn't argue. She slid a chair out and flopped down into it. Terrence frowned at the seat next to her, reached for it, and pulled his own chair out.

"I see you spent some time with a necromancer," the innkeeper said as she set a mug down in front of Vicky and put the other by an empty chair. She walked around the table and lifted a small bottle out of an ancient spice rack. She unscrewed the top, and put a sprinkle of brown dust in each mug. The spice bottle clicked back into place and the innkeeper joined them at the table. Jasper purred on Vicky's shoulder, and the innkeeper stirred her mug.

"You've come to tell me about Damian."

The warmth in Vicky's chest, that feeling of coming home, fled in a heartbeat. Her grip tightened around the warm mug, trying to recapture some of that contented feeling, but it was gone. At least she still had the warmth of the hot chocolate. She took a sip, savoring the smooth rich flavor. "It's not good."

"I think it's the best hot chocolate you can find in Missouri," the innkeeper said, raising an eyebrow.

Vicky laughed despite herself. "That's not what I meant."

"I know dear. Damian's knee-deep in a shit storm."

Vicky's eyebrows drew together. "He ... merged

with Hern. I can't explain it. But the thing he's walking around as, it's like the Old Man. But it's bigger, taller."

The innkeeper flexed her fingers on the table. "It is a risk for every son of Anubis. But for Damian to walk the same lands as Leviticus … it brings a sadness to my heart."

"What can we do?" Vicky asked. "Damian said to bring you the backpack."

Both of the innkeeper's eyebrows rose at that. "He … spoke to you? Even in his current state?"

"To me," Terrence said, drawing the innkeeper's attention. "Vicky touched my arm on the battlefield, and that woke me up. That's the only way I can put it. I was following the other ghosts blindly, with only flashes of self-awareness. But she broke whatever spell it was."

"Did you hit him with a soulart?" the innkeeper asked.

"You mean stab him with a soulsword?" Vicky asked. "No. Would that work on a ghost?"

She eyed Terrence, and the ghost fidgeted.

"That's not the kind of thing we try out on our friends," the innkeeper said. "What happened then?"

"I followed him," Terrence said. He shrugged, as if not knowing how else to describe it. "There was a golden light on the back of the colossus, on Damian's back. I followed him and when I reached that light I had another vision. That's when he told me to get the backpack to Vicky. To tell Vicky to get the backpack to you. And so we're here."

"Let me see," the innkeeper said.

Vicky slid her the backpack, cut straps and all. The slowly drying fabric left a damp trail behind it.

The innkeeper methodically unzipped each pouch and glanced inside. "Moon pies," she muttered. "Beef jerky! What is wrong with that boy?" She whispered a few more colorful things under her breath before she unzipped the main pouch.

A crease formed in her brow and she turned the pack to Vicky. "Would you be a dear and take Gaia's hand out for me?"

Vicky nodded and grabbed the gray flesh. She set it on the table next to her cocoa before taking another sip of the warm drink.

The innkeeper pulled out a handful of speed loaders, some stray bullets, and Damian's pepperbox. It didn't have the holster, which meant he must still be wearing it, or at least it was still with him, buried underneath that mountain of gravemakers.

The thought made Vicky shiver, and she was glad for the warmth of the hot chocolate.

"There's not much here," the innkeeper said. "Just

Gaia's hand …" The innkeeper narrowed her eyes at the gray flesh.

"What is it?" Terrence asked, obviously picking up on something Vicky hadn't noticed.

"The hand. He wanted you to bring the hand here." The innkeeper took a sip of her drink before pulling a flask from an inside pocket of her denim shirt. Instead of answering, she took a long swig and grimaced. Her words came out in an exasperated drawl, "He's *mad*."

Before Vicky could ask why she thought Damian was mad, or what she thought Damian had cooked up, the crack of a branch against the rear window behind the table echoed through the room. The innkeeper gestured and the window slid open.

That was new. Vicky hadn't seen the innkeeper use that kind of magic so casually before. Beyond the window crouched Stump. Only his face was fully visible, the rest of his body outside of the window frame.

"Someone approaches," Stump said.

"Friend or foe?" The innkeeper asked.

"Hard to say," Stump said, tapping the edge of his vine-formed beard. "He has been both, and he rides upon a reaper. Older than Jasper, and perhaps as ancient as the horned Beast of Gorias himself."

"Drake." The innkeeper stood up, took another

swig out of her flask, and angrily screwed the top closed. "Let's see what the bastard wants."

"Don't attack him," Vicky said. "He still ... He's still our friend."

"Girl," the innkeeper said, "if there's one thing I've learned in my life here, it's that you don't attack a knight riding a reaper."

The innkeeper grumbled about needing to get another mug because she'd only planned on one guest that evening. She gestured at the cupboard and the glass door slid open before an old terra-cotta mug floated down to the counter.

"I'll feed that fairy some sugar. We'll see how that goes." She muttered something else under her breath as she stomped down the hallway, but Vicky couldn't make it out.

She exchanged a glance with Terrence, and the ghost blew out a long breath before looking around the room. "This place is amazing."

"I guess it is," Vicky said.

The quiet squeak of one of the door's hinges reached them before Drake's voice echoed through the house. "Is she here?"

Vicky didn't hear the innkeeper's reply, but the footsteps coming down the hallway were distinct. Two people, one armored. Vicky wondered what the innkeeper would do if Drake's boots scratched the floor. The thought of watching that exchange pulled her lips up into an evil grin.

"… she safe?" Drake asked before they rounded the corner.

"Of course, of course," the innkeeper said. "She came here with her reaper, and the ghost. And a hand." The last phrase she said with an ominous undertone to the words. "You could have sent her through the Ways. The same way you got here. Through Columbia and she could have flown the rest of the way. Why didn't you?"

"Of course," Drake said as they rounded the corner. "That *would* have been my suggestion if the wolves hadn't interfered." There was a tightness in his brow, a concern that Vicky hadn't seen very often. It loosened when he saw her, and the rigidness of his back relaxed a fraction.

"You're safe."

CHAPTER THIRTEEN

"YOU HAD DOUBTS?" Vicky asked.

Drake's expression fell. Something warred across his face. The relief he'd shown when he first entered the room turned darker, angrier.

"What were you thinking?" Drake snapped. "Using the hand of glory? Taking the word of that werewolf?"

Before Vicky could so much as respond, the innkeeper held up her free hand as she finished pouring. She picked up the now-steaming mug from the counter and thrust it into Drake's grip. "Drink this before you say things you'll regret."

Drake eyed the innkeeper.

"Sit down or I will sit you down." The innkeeper's easy but firm manner crossed over into something else. It was a warning, of that Vicky had no doubt.

Drake hesitated for a moment, and then slid a chair out at the table and sat down in his full-size form beside Terrence. "The hand was too much of a risk." Drake set his mug down on the table with a click. "It could have killed you."

"There are a lot of things that could have killed me," Vicky said. "Some of them did."

"Are you really willing to put your parents through that again?"

Vicky felt the anger welling up in her gut. She wanted to scream at Drake, tear him up one side and down the other, but the rage kept the words from forming. Instead her hands turned into fists and she started to rise out of her chair.

"That's enough," the innkeeper said. "You two are casting barbs at each other, but that's not why we're here. That's not why Damian sent you here, and that's certainly not what your friends need out of you."

"Too big of a risk," Drake muttered.

"A calculated risk. But she's here, and she's alive, and you need to better learn how to control your emotions." When Drake and Vicky both fell silent, the innkeeper continued. "Now then, that wolf, as you so casually called him, is Wahya. He's one of the oldest werewolves I know of in this country. Perhaps the world. I suspect Hugh is one of his few elders. So while yes, Wahya may have only had a theory, a hypothesis, it was founded in centuries of experience. If not millennia. Wolves do not live that long a life without a level of cunning few can understand."

If she was baiting Drake with that comment, he didn't rise to it. Instead he sipped from the mug, picked up a marshmallow from the center of the table, and plopped it into his hot chocolate.

"I'm glad you're safe," Vicky said.

Drake raised his eyes to meet hers. "Me? I was never at risk."

"Never at risk?" Terrence blurted out. "That horned dragon you were fighting looked like it could tear your own beast in half."

"She's not a beast. She's a reaper."

Terrence shook his head. "As you say, but that was a full army in the skies behind us. And that dragon could've run you down."

Drake twisted the mug between his hands and took another sip.

"He's right," Vicky said. "You know he's right."

"You shouldn't have taken your reaper away from that battle," Drake said, anger seeping into his words. "The entire thing, this ghost," he said, gesturing to Terrence, "your flight from the battle. What were you thinking?"

"I was thinking I didn't want me, Sam, and Damian to die," Vicky snapped. "I was thinking Damian has a plan to fight this and I need to help him."

The shadow in the window moved, and Stump

spoke. "She is young, but she is wise. Even a Demon Sword can see that, blinded as he may be by his own confidence and loyalty. Which begs the question, where do your loyalties lie?"

The innkeeper watched Drake, and Vicky almost missed the slight raise of her eyebrows. Apparently, she wasn't the only one who was surprised Stump had so bluntly questioned Drake's loyalties.

It was Vicky who answered. "He's my friend. He's saved me more than once. I trust him."

"Let the fairy answer for himself," the innkeeper said, offering a small smile.

Drake leaned forward in the chair, his wings flexing as he rested his forearms on the table. "For many years, I was loyal to the king, and only the king." Drake stared into his mug as if the dark liquid were showing him memories he might not care to have. "We masked the king's descent into madness as long as we could. Hid the murders and mad machinations like you can't imagine. But the king always cared for his inner circle. So even in the end, when his personality fractured, and he concocted an insane plan, we supported him.

"It wasn't until Gettysburg, until Falias was ripped from Faerie. When he brought the city here to kill countless commoners, and the disregard for the Fae who remained in the city was a nightmare to behold.

But I don't think I need to tell you the rest. I don't think I need to tell you about the girl who sits across the table from me who pulled those Fae through the Abyss. Who saved the lives of thousands, even as our king, our *protector*, was willing to sacrifice every last soul."

"And what's in it for you?" the innkeeper asked. "Redemption?"

Drake slowly shook his head. "I do not need redemption. I served my kingdom well. As it should be. But even if that was my goal, I know I will not find it. So I will help who I can, to secure the future of my people, and hers." He said the last with a nod toward Vicky. "But it's hard when my closest allies flee a pivotal battle." Drake locked eyes with Vicky.

Vicky squeezed her mug. "I'm not going to apologize for that. You always taught me to seize an opportunity when I saw it, and so I did. Damian reached out through Terrence, through me, and that's why we're here. I couldn't have planned it because I didn't know it was going to happen."

"Plans are shit once they meet the enemy," Terrence said, and the cadence to his voice made it sound like he was recalling a long-forgotten quote.

"A sentiment shared by the Fae," Drake said, crossing his arms. "Be more careful when you can. If you, or

Samantha, or Damian do not survive this … I will not be the one to face Zola if that happens."

At that a wicked grin crossed the innkeeper's face. "At least you learned something in the last few years."

Drake's armor started clicking under the table when he unfolded his arms. Vicky leaned over to see him bouncing his knee like her dad tended to when he had a bit too much coffee. The sugar was getting to him, and she suppressed a grin.

"Shut up, kid," Drake growled.

"I didn't say a thing."

"He handles it better than Foster," the innkeeper said.

"No doubt," Vicky said. "Did you hear what they did in Damian's coffee cup?"

"That's not something I care to dwell on." The innkeeper held up her hand. "Yes, I've heard the story. I prefer not to remember it."

"What?" Terrence asked.

"Don't ask," the innkeeper muttered. "Just be glad it wasn't any of the mugs we're drinking hot cocoa out of."

Drake frowned at the innkeeper for a second and then took another sip of his drink. Terrence remained silent. Apparently he'd been around the supernaturals enough to know when he should listen to their advice and when he shouldn't.

Jasper rolled down Vicky's arm and plopped onto the table next to her mug. He vibrated and purred, sending ripples through the hot cocoa.

"Why send us here?" Vicky asked. "Why did Damian want me to come here? And bring you that?" she said with a nod to the backpack.

"Because he's mad," the innkeeper said. "But he might be right."

CHAPTER FOURTEEN

D RAKE FROWNED AND glanced between Vicky and the innkeeper. "What do you mean?"

"I mean Damian has come up with a plan. As compromised as he is, he's trying to save his sister, Vicky, and whoever else stands in his way. I believe the reason Damian sent you here is because of that." The innkeeper gestured toward the hand of Gaia.

"This?" Vicky asked, picking up the hand of glory. "For what? All this does is let you walk in the Abyss. What can Gaia do?"

Drake cursed.

The innkeeper nodded. "She can do exactly what you said. Gaia can walk into the Abyss, but it is not the only thing she can do. She can also pull people into the Abyss, transport them to other places, other realms, or trap monsters in an eternal darkness."

The pieces snapped together in Vicky's mind, and judging how the innkeeper looked away from her, Vicky hadn't hidden her expression of horror at the thought. But would it work? Could she convince Gaia to pull Damian into the Abyss?

"You want to lock him away?" Vicky said.

The innkeeper shook her head. "It's not me. This is Damian's idea. And it might work. If he's trapped in the time loops of the Abyss, the channels his powers have carved through the Seals should be enough to keep you and Sam alive."

"Alive for what?" Vicky asked. "He'll be trapped in darkness. That's monstrous."

"And he'll be locked away with monsters," Terrence said. "You saw the things in there, didn't you? That wasn't just something I saw as a ghost?"

"You saw the leviathans of the Abyss?" the innkeeper asked. "That is not an unusual vision for the dead to have there I would think. Leviathans are flesh and bone, and there are darker things hidden in that place: Old Gods, and older things, and gateways for the eldritch."

"You really think it's possible to trap him there?" Drake asked.

The innkeeper frowned. "The fact that it is possible doesn't mean it is likely to work for long. The exposure to the powers inside that place, inside that nothingness, may be the end of him. But there is more to consider. It is not only Damian, Sam, and Vicky who would be put at risk. It would put Gaia's life at risk to drag that kind of power into the darkness, to lock it away into the Abyss, and pin it down where it can do no harm."

"That could kill you," Stump said, drawing their attention back to the open window. The vines of his beard shifted, and the branches that formed his face drew into a frown. "You are our last tie to the goddess. We cannot lose her and you. Our people are already fractured, and hope is sparse in these dark times. Do not extinguish that light."

The innkeeper almost growled. "You say too much. But what is the alternative? Leave the boy to die? Leave him in Nudd's hands? To carry out whatever madness he intends?"

"We still have the Old Man," Drake said. "Perhaps he could …"

"Perhaps he could what?" the innkeeper snapped. "Perhaps he could kill Damian? And kill Vicky in the same blow? We lose the alliance with the vampires if Sam dies, and that is no small thing. You've seen enough war, enough empires fall in your long life to understand where this ends."

Drake's bouncing foot stopped. He almost sagged into his chair, the tips of his wings curling over.

"What did Stump mean this could hurt you?" Vicky asked.

The innkeeper's jaw flexed. She frowned, lines deepening on her forehead before she took a deep breath. "Think of me as an anchor for Gaia in this realm, for the body of the Titan buried beneath this home. I am bound to her, and she to me."

"Is that why you never leave the mansion?" Vicky asked.

"I leave sometimes," the innkeeper said.

"But I've only ever seen you on the grounds," Vicky said.

"The grounds aren't technically in the mansion."

Vicky grimaced at the innkeeper. "That's a technicality."

"As you get older, you'll find technicalities are quite important."

"I didn't have to get very old to discover that," Vicky muttered.

The innkeeper looked around the group. "Rest here. The rooms are vacant on the third floor. I have guests on the second, but they won't bother you so long as you don't bother them. I need to ponder this. I'm not sure I've fully considered all of the repercussions if we go through with Damian's ... plan."

"Ask Zola," Vicky said.

"This is somewhat beyond even Zola's skills," the innkeeper said.

"But it's Damian. She's his master, his mentor. She's family. Ask her."

The innkeeper drummed her fingernails on the table.

"We don't have time to stay here," Drake said.

The innkeeper didn't even hesitate when she saw her opportunity. "Rest here for a few hours and I'll promise to contact Zola."

Drake's mouth hung open for a second before it snapped shut. He narrowed his eyes and put an impressive amount of irritation into a single sharp nod.

Vicky frowned, ground her teeth, and then agreed. "Fine."

"It is good you are staying," Stump said. "There are a few who would like to meet you. If you would come outside, to the back, I would introduce you before you rest."

"Go," the innkeeper said. "I'll clean up."

"Thank you for your hospitality," Terrence said.

The innkeeper placed a hand over her heart. "A guest with manners. It's been so long."

Vicky laughed and dragged Drake up out of his chair, much to his protests. She quickly stuffed the hand of Gaia back into the backpack before hanging it on the back of the chair. She pulled Drake down the hall and out the side door onto the deck that wrapped around the house.

Vicky stepped out into the yard beside Stump. As tall as he was, the green man was almost dwarfed by the companion at his side.

Stump gestured to the second green man. "This is Whip. Whip thought of taking another name, such as that the commoners have given, but a name like Weeping, or Willow didn't have the same undertones that we have come to favor in our names."

"I can feel the goddess through her," Whip said. This green man's features were more delicate, almost feminine, and the more Whip spoke, Vicky realized she was just that. "We've always been able the sense the presence of the goddess here. I am sure you know why. But it is more like an echo, a thing nearly forgotten. But through you, the goddess pulses. I have only felt the like one other time."

Stump's agreement was like the rumble of thunder. "Only in Damian. And there is great irony there. That a deathspeaker would be so bound to our goddess."

It was then Vicky realized Whip wasn't the only green man standing in the backyard. Other trunks moved, and dark eyes opened and closed in the bark. Subtle movements, the kind a commoner might miss, or write off as a breeze. Vicky made out at least two more figures, but there could have been more. A crooked and twisted old trunk walked beneath the hanging branches of Whip. The green man leaned on a kind of cane formed from an ancient black wood. He came to rest with one bark-laden hand on top of the other, his weight borne by the cane.

"I have seen this light before," the old green man said.

"Who are you?" Vicky asked.

But before she finished asking the question, Drake had stepped up beside her. It looked like a casual move, but she didn't miss how close his hand had come to the hilt of his sword. Drake felt threatened, or thought she was threatened, but Vicky didn't sense it at all.

"I have no mortal name," the old green man said.

"We call him Stub," Stump said.

"I do not answer to that name," Stub said.

"Stub?" Vicky said, perplexed by the word. Stump kind of made sense. Whip was incredibly obvious. "Why Stub?"

"It is short for Stubborn," Stump said. "For he is stubborn as one of the great trees far to the northwest. So his own stubbornness gave us the idea to call him Stubborn. But he complained that the name was too long, so we shortened it."

"That's … unfortunate." Vicky's eyebrow rose a little higher. "Why don't you just name him after those trees? You're talking about sequoias right?"

The old green man cocked his head to the side.

"Should've named him Ironic," the innkeeper said, settling into a chair on the back deck.

Whip's expression drew up into a smile, and Vicky was already starting to like the only female green man she'd ever met.

Sequoia watched the innkeeper for a moment before saying, "I've seen this power before. Do you know where?" His eyes swept down to Drake. "It was in your master. It ran through the Mad King after he murdered our goddess."

Drake shifted his weight, his wings tensing up in a flash.

"Do not!" the innkeeper snapped. She was on her feet in an instant. "Neither of you attack. These are old wounds. You must not let them divide us now."

A glint of moonlight showed on the blade of Drake's sword where he'd already drawn it halfway out of the sheath. But it wasn't the only weapon that had come into play. Sequoia stood with something like a mace his hands. Four vines came down and tied into heavy-looking blocks of wood. Six spines shot through the bark, and Vicky had little doubt of how much damage one blow from Sequoia's mace could do.

"Sometimes old scores don't need to be settled,"

Drake said. He hesitated and then slammed his sword back into its sheath.

Sequoia inclined his head slightly, his brows drawing together in a plain expression of anger. His hands flexed, and the mace-like weapon vanished into the gnarled wood of his arms.

"I will tie every last one of you up," Whip said. "Behave yourselves. You act as impulsive as the commoners."

Sequoia blew out a disgusted breath. He raised a hand to his forehead, and muttered, "Maybe I *am* losing my mind. Or perhaps I have a better perspective of how bad things are for our people."

"You have my allegiance," Drake said. "If my word is good enough, then understand that my bond with this child aligns our goals."

"I'm not a child," Vicky said, unable to keep the exasperation from her voice.

"I am but a child," Stump said, "when compared to the age of Sequoia."

The older green men inclined his head. "So be it. We can settle our differences at some other date. If we all survive what's coming."

The innkeeper slapped the arms of her chair. "Your rooms are ready. Vicky, you can have the Nile. You're welcome to take the opposite room, Drake. Or you can stay down here on the couch if you'd prefer."

Drake hesitated. "Can my dragon enter your home?"

"She's already taken to one of the rooms. You'll find her waiting for you."

"Go in peace," Whip said. "Until peace would put your loved ones at risk."

They said good night to the green men, and Vicky headed back inside Rivercene, wondering if she'd be able to sleep before she heard Zola's thoughts on Damian's plan.

But restless thoughts weren't the only thing wandering the halls of Rivercene.

CHAPTER FIFTEEN

VICKY TOOK THE rear staircase. She slid past the old piano and up a few creaky steps to the second floor. She circled the banister and eyed an old quilt framed on the wall before hurrying up the stairs to the third floor. To call those stairs narrow would be an understatement. She could hardly believe Damian would be able to fit his gangly feet on them. Even with one hand on the banister, she didn't have to raise her arm far to reach the other wall.

Something clicked nearby in the house, like a door closing, but with the strange acoustics, Vicky couldn't identify where it came from. She frowned and looked around for Terrence, only to find that she couldn't see the ghost. "Are you still there, Terrence?"

She heard footsteps on the stairs she'd just come from, but no one was there. As she watched, a shadowy form resolved at the bottom step. It was Terrence, but he was more transparent than she'd seen him before.

Vicky frowned at the ghost. "What happened?"

"The house is warded," Terrence said. "I think if I stay close to you it doesn't have as heavy effect on me. Or maybe it was because we came from the Abyss?"

"You'll be okay?"

Terrence studied the hallway. "Innkeeper said it's safe. I must admit I've never seen a wardstone before. The innkeeper's full of stories. I'll be downstairs if you need me."

Vicky nodded and continued down the hall. She turned to the left, and at the far end beneath the window she could see an overstuffed bookshelf. Each of the rooms had a little nameplate by it. She could make out the details of some of the couches and recliners as she neared the reading nook. She found the Nile room near the end.

As soon as she reached for the knob, the lock clicked and the door swung open. A deep blue paint and exposed brick work framed by carefully sanded wood greeted her. A shiny brass bedframe stood out in the dim light, and an ancient wardrobe flanked her by the door. Beyond that was a small table with leaves folded down so it was barely two feet wide. Vicky passed it, running a hand along the aged wood before she poked her head into the bathroom. A giant whirlpool tub waited, and an old pedestal sink sat beside it by the toilet.

As tempting as a bath was, the bed was more enticing. Vicky chose to rinse her face and arms in the sink and call it a night. A good measure of dirt and blood came off her face, and she frowned at the stains she left behind on the innkeeper's towels.

Considering who the innkeeper tended to have as guests, Vicky figured she'd have an effective stain remover. Vicky made her way back to the bed, slid her phone out of her pocket, and flopped onto her back. She picked up an old book from the nightstand.

Vicky wasn't sure exactly how long she managed to stay awake reading about pirates and privateers, but she knew it hadn't been long. The battle had worn her down, and the thought of things to come made sleep fleeting. But it was the thundering knock at her door that startled her awake.

As soon as her eyes opened, and she slid the book to the side, only silence remained. The knock sounded again, but this time it didn't seem so loud. This time it was followed by a small voice that asked, "Are you awake?"

Vicky yawned and padded over to the door. She reached for the handle, the lock clicked, and she pulled the door open. Vicky came face to face with a death bat. Which seemed an odd name for the cute upside-down stubby-nosed pale puffball frowning at her.

"You're not Damian," the death bat said.

A small smile crawled across Vicky's face. "Luna." Vicky had heard stories from Zola about the fluffy white murder machine.

The bat cocked her head and then dropped from the ceiling. She landed in near silence when her feet touched the floor. "I thought I heard the innkeeper say Damian was here."

"Damian's ... in trouble," Vicky said. As silly as she felt hiding a hard truth from a creature called a death bat, she couldn't come right out and tell Luna how much trouble Damian was in. But that didn't feel right. It felt like a knot tightening in her chest as she remembered some of the things that Damian himself had kept from Vicky. Memory after memory came back to her from the moment she made up her mind not to tell the death bat. The truth about what happened to her, her rebirth, the separation from the Destroyer, everything right down to the bond she now shared with him and Sam.

"What happened?" Luna asked, her eyes widening.

Vicky's resolution cracked. "Come on in. You deserve to know."

Luna's ears twitched back and forth and she wrung her clawed hands together before she bobbed her head and followed Vicky into the Nile room.

Vicky had heard the tales about Luna, and the contribution she'd made to the battle at Meramec Caverns against the dark-touched. But the thought of this little puffball killing anything, much less a dark-touched vampire, was almost impossible to reconcile in her mind. Vicky wondered if that's how people thought of her. They saw the child, the teenager, and her potential. But her threat? That they were blind to.

"What's happened to him?" Luna asked.

Vicky took a deep breath, and she let the story flow. She didn't hide the details from Luna, not even after the death bat winced, or turned away. She clicked her claws together as Vicky told her of the fight in Falias, and the confrontation with Hern, and how they'd lost Damian.

"But there's still hope?"

Hope. It was nice to think there was always hope, but sometimes that was hard to remember when the darkness had its claws around your throat. But Vicky didn't say that aloud. Instead, she only nodded.

The door clicked open and Vicky frowned at the empty hall. Jasper rolled in, his gray fur surging and stretching as he bounced up onto the table and looked up at Luna. She reached a hand out to the reaper, and Jasper purred when she scratched him between the eyes.

"He needs Camazotz," Luna said. "Camazotz can beat anyone."

But that wasn't entirely true, Vicky knew. Camazotz had almost died in one of the battles with the harbinger at Greenville.

"He's done enough," Vicky said. "You've lost enough of your brothers and sisters. He's right to protect them."

A wry grin lifted the corner of Luna's mouth. "You don't know where he's at, do you?"

Vicky frowned at the bat. "Why?"

"He's fighting the dark-touched beside Hugh in Kansas City." Luna shook her head. "Werewolves and the death bats of Camazotz side by side."

"Why now?" Vicky asked. "Why is he there?"

"Almost the entire Kansas City pack was destroyed by the dark-touched. He's been taking care of the stragglers, and trying to keep the dark-touched away from what's left."

What's left, not *who's* left. Vicky frowned at the words. "And what is left?"

Luna shrugged. "They don't tell me everything. All I know is it's important. And apparently powerful enough that Camazotz thought it was worth the risk." She scratched at Jasper and the furball trilled. "Camazotz forbade me to join them, so I came here. I like it here. The innkeeper is nice, and it's … peaceful. Like when the death bats find a remote home, where everything leaves us alone. I thought we might have that in Greenville. But we didn't."

Luna's smile slowly fell. "And now Damian? I like him."

"Me too."

Vicky ruffled Jasper's fur and a decision solidified in her mind. "Have you ever walked through the Abyss?"

CHAPTER SIXTEEN

VICKY AND LUNA made their way downstairs a short time later. Vicky felt a bond to the young death bat, a shared struggle both in what they'd survived, and in how their peers still perceived them.

"But I'm telling you," Luna said. "If you ever get to Kansas City, there's this little place called RJ's Bob-Be-Que Shack. You've never had anything like it."

Vicky grinned as their footsteps echoed down the stairs. "I can see why you got along with Damian."

"I've heard the stories," Luna said. "He's a bottom-less pit."

"Just wait until his metabolism stops working," Vicky said. "He's gonna be like a house!"

Luna laughed.

But that might not happen. For all she knew, Damian might not live through the night, and she might not either.

They walked in silence for a while, Vicky catching hints of gray shadows at the edge of her vision. But nothing resolved, nothing solidified. A small haze of dim orbs flickered by an old wheelchair, weaving themselves between the old wicker back. The sight settled on Vicky like a weight, the fact she might never see her parents grow old enough to need that kind of care, or to kick Damian's ass hard enough that he needed to live in one for a few months.

Their footsteps fell heavier, and a moment later Luna's claws caught her arm.

"It'll be okay," Luna said. "I promise."

No one could promise something like that. Vicky looked back at the young death bat, and she knew she wasn't hiding the sadness in her eyes. She knew it was plain to see, but she was still alive, and as long as she drew breath, she wouldn't sit idly by.

Luna cocked her head to the side. She looked down the grand staircase and frowned. "Did you hear that?"

"Hear what?"

"On the TV. They're talking about Falias. Come on!"

Luna hopped into the air and spread her arms. There was enough resistance she glided gently to land in front of the front door. She vanished into the great room before Vicky had even made it halfway down the stairs. Luna's hearing was clearly infinitely better than Vicky's own. It wasn't until she reached the bottom that she heard the whisper of the television.

She made her way around the corner and saw the old television set flashing in the corner with the innkeeper and Terrence sitting in front of it. The spires of Falias filled the screen while banners of stock exchanges Vicky cared nothing about lined up across the bottom. But as the camera panned, and she saw the massive silhouette of the colossus etched against the glowing lights of Falias, her stomach sank.

"Luna! Luna?" the innkeeper asked. "I thought you were sleeping."

"I thought I heard you say Damian was here. But that's ..." She trailed off and stared at the television. She pointed at the colossus. "Is that Damian?"

"I'm afraid so," Terrence said. He turned toward Vicky and Luna, and much to his credit, he stifled a bark of surprise. "You're like the bats from Greenville? The ones who tried to help Dirge?"

Luna nodded, but she didn't take her eyes off the television.

The innkeeper groaned. "Luna, Terrence, Terrence, Luna. Terrence is friends with Dirge, the old forest god who the lives in Greenville."

The reporter on the screen brought the conversation in the room to a halt. "You heard it here first. The Fae king's monster will begin executing prisoners at dawn. Spies from the terrorist organization known as the Obsidian Inn will, and I quote, face justice at the hands of their executioner."

"Damian would never do that," Luna said. "What's happening? How did they get control over him?" She turned to Vicky. "I thought you said he was still fighting back?"

"He was," Vicky said, the words hollow in her own head. She stared at the television. The reporter's words flowed around her as if they hadn't been spoken. Damian was losing himself. If they didn't get to them, could he survive this? Could any of them?

"That certainly cocks things up," the innkeeper snapped. She froze, her eyes flashing to Vicky and then Luna. "You don't tell any of the adults I said that in front of you."

Vicky narrowed her eyes. "Sometimes I feel like you people have never even met Damian."

The innkeeper's lips twitched. It was then that the front doorbell rang. It wasn't a slow chime of a patient person, but the rapid pulse of someone twisting the knob as fast as they could. The innkeeper stared at the door for a time before a slow smile spread across her face.

The ringing of the bell was joined by the crash of something against the front door. Three quick strikes, one long, and three more quick strikes.

"Get the door," the innkeeper said, looking at Vicky. "I'll put the tea on."

Vicky watched the innkeeper stand up and walk back toward the kitchen. She exchanged a glance with Luna and then headed for the front door. The loud bangs crashed against the door again and Vicky could just make out grumbled muttering on the other side.

She opened the door and almost caught the head of a knobby cane with her face before Zola pulled up short.

"Didn't anyone ever tell you to announce yourself, girl?" The old Cajun pushed in past Vicky, gently nudging her out of the way while somehow providing a little assurance with a quick squeeze of her arm.

"She's in the kitchen," Vicky said.

Zola pulled her hood down, letting the silver gray charms and her braids tinkle as she walked.

Terrence trailed Zola. The closer he got to the necromancer and Vicky, the more corporeal he seemed.

"I can see Terrence better here," Vicky said. "He was faded upstairs."

Terrence exchanged a nod with Zola when she glanced back at him.

"Is your wardstone acting up?" Zola shouted as she rounded the corner.

"Has been for a while. I'd say the last two weeks at least."

Zola growled and took the steaming mug from the innkeeper. "Makes me wonder what the hell Mike is up to. Or is it Ward we should be more worried about?"

"Or Damian's connection to Gaia?" The innkeeper asked.

Zola nodded and took a sip of her tea. "It's an interesting thought. If you've seen anomalies before yesterday, Ah suspect something else. You're still well-guarded?"

The innkeeper inclined her head. "We still have many green men on the grounds. Stump's people. Good people who will do what they can to protect Gaia."

Vicky couldn't stay silent anymore. She heard the armored boots coming down the stairs behind her and the pale brown ball of fur that was Drake's dragon squeaking at her heels. She frowned, wondering where Jasper had gotten off to, before the other dragon appeared beside Drake's at her feet. Vicky stared at Zola and the words tumbled out in a torrent.

"We have to take the hand of Gaia back to Falias. Get Gaia to take Damian into the Abyss and lock him away there until we can figure out something else."

Zola stared at Vicky for a short time before shaking

her head. "That's mad, girl."

"You have a better idea?" The innkeeper asked.

"Perhaps one that won't kill all three of them?" Zola said, biting off the words. "Let me see what Ah can think of."

"I'm afraid the timeline has been shortened for any plans," the innkeeper said.

"What do you mean?"

The innkeeper told Zola about the coverage, and how Damian had become Nudd's executioner. They had until morning, or Damian would have far more blood on his hands.

Zola cursed. "Then no. Ah don't have a better idea."

The innkeeper steepled her fingers.

"Shit," Zola snapped. "If Samantha has heard about this, there's no telling what she might do." Zola slid her phone out of her pocket. She flipped through her contacts and then put the phone on speaker. A few rings, and a world of tension, and all that answered was a generic repeat of the phone number Zola had dialed.

"God damn it, girl." Zola's fingers tapped the screen, and she sent a text faster than Vicky's own parents could.

Nothing came back.

"Let me try," Vicky said. "She might respond to me.

She won't want to hurt me."

Zola eyed Vicky, and gave her a nod.

Drake stood silently behind Vicky. If he had a protest, he kept it to himself, his arms crossed and his mouth shut.

The dragons nuzzled Vicky's ankles as she tapped out a text of her own. It was only three words.

"Don't kill me."

CHAPTER SEVENTEEN

ZOLA'S GAZE ROSE from the short message Vicky had typed into her phone and met her eyes. "Jesus girl."

"I know …" Vicky started to explain, but her phone rang, and the image of a ferret with long vampire teeth on the screen showed her it was Sam.

Vicky took a deep breath and put the phone on speaker. "Hey, Sam."

"Kid," Sam said. But her voice fractured, and the shaky breath on the other end of the line was plain to hear. "Kid, we're not going to make it through. I've got this. I'm sorry."

"What are you talking about?" Vicky asked.

Something thumped, a hollow knock, and the crash of heavy wood boomed over the speaker. Vicky frowned at the screen, wondering what in the hell Sam was doing.

"Samantha, where are you?" Zola asked.

Sam's voice was still shaky when she responded.

"I'm at the shop. Going to end this, Zola. I love you. Tell my parents." Her voice cracked, and the slight rise in tone almost made it a question.

Zola looked angry for a moment, but it passed as she spoke. "The least you can do is give them a phone call. They deserve that, Samantha."

Ever so faint, the sound of a knife being ripped from its sheath echoed over the speaker.

"What is that?" Vicky asked, looking up at Zola.

Zola growled.

"Goodbye," Sam said. "I'm putting an end to this."

The line went dead. The home screen on Vicky's phone flashed up, and she felt lost.

"What's she doing?" Luna asked.

"She was in the chest." Zola glanced at Vicky and then Luna. "She has the *splendorum mortem*. She is going to kill her brother."

"Well," the innkeeper said. "It seems Damian's rather insane plan of having Gaia drag him into the Abyss might be the better of two options at this point. Shit."

"We should be finding a way to spare Vicky from that fool. You risk us all to save one man," Drake said. "To save Nudd's *tool*."

Zola grimaced at Drake. "The only tool in this situation is *you*. Servant of the Mad King for millennia.

Ah won't kill you, unless you get in the way, but hold your tongue."

As fast as Vicky usually was to defend Drake, the idea of letting Damian die without even trying to save him turned her stomach. Could Drake really do that if it was one of his allies? Damian was technically an ally, but to say they had a rocky partnership was a gross understatement.

"Do you have any way to intercept Samantha?" the innkeeper asked.

"We can track her phone," Vicky said.

Zola shook her head. "She's too smart for that. She'll either leave the phone at the shop or the Pit, or destroy it altogether. Did you not hear her voice? She's already made up her mind. And Ah understand why she has."

Objectively, Vicky understood too. But if they lost Damian, Sam died too. Vicky died. The thought of dying again wasn't the worst part. The thought of letting her friends down, the people who had walked into the Burning Lands to free her from the Destroyer, the friends who had died to save her. That was what she couldn't let come to pass.

"So we have no way of finding her," Drake said. "But we know where she will be. If she truly has that demon blade as you say, there's only one place she will go."

"Falias," Zola said.

But something clicked in the back of Vicky's mind. "If Sam was truly set on just killing him, she would've killed herself with that dagger. That would take all three of us down in one strike. What the hell is she doing?"

Vicky dialed Sam's number again but no one answered.

"Then we find her and get the dagger," Drake said. "You two walk with Gaia and I'll meet you at the Obsidian Inn. If there's anything left."

"I'm coming with you," Terrence said, tossing Damian's backpack over his shoulder where he managed to tie the two separate straps together. "We don't leave our friends behind."

Zola frowned at the ghost. "Ah think you've been around these people too long, Terrence. Just a bit too long."

Drake blew out an exasperated breath. "If you want to risk yourself, I won't stop you. But we're going up against a level of necromancy few people have witnessed and survived. It's more dangerous for a ghost than most."

"I'll keep an eye on him," Luna said, puffing up her chest. Her fur bristled until she looked almost as fluffy as Jasper. Vicky suspected that wasn't the intended effect, but she also wanted Luna to come with her. As much power as she'd gained, as much as she'd learned, it was still easier to face your enemy with friends, and she already felt a kinship with the puffball.

"There is another way," Stump said, his voice echoing from the open window.

The innkeeper turned slowly toward the green man. "Stump, I know what you're going to—"

"You could awaken the goddess. Re-unite the hand and let her bless the necromancer with the gift of the woods." Stump focused on the innkeeper. "Many believe her resurrection is nigh, and Damian has twisted Fae magicks more than once to bring death where there should be life. There is no reason not to use death to bring life where it has gone dormant."

The innkeeper shook her head. "No. Gaia has offered her gifts before. The risk is too great, and I believe Damian understood that." She grimaced and looked to Zola.

The old Cajun eyed the innkeeper. "If we stop Samantha, it may be worth the risk."

"It is not so simple," the innkeeper said. "Gaia would need powers that have been lost for millennia. Regardless, we don't have the time now. Go, save Damian from his sister if you can, and try not to let him kill you."

"Come," Drake said. The tan ball of fur rolled away from Vicky's ankle and vanished out the front door with the Demon Sword.

"Go with them," the innkeeper said to Luna. "But if Camazotz asks, I had nothing to do with this."

Luna threw her arms around the old woman, the flesh of her wings stretching out a bit before she released the innkeeper.

"Then we get back to the fight," Zola said.

Vicky pulled the hand of glory out of the backpack. "Don't let go."

Zola wrapped her hand around Vicky's arm, and Luna took the other.

Terrence hooked his arm in Zola's and took a deep breath. "All I know is I don't like roller coasters."

The innkeeper gave him a perplexed look as Vicky laced her fingers into Gaia's, and they stepped into the Abyss. But for a moment, just before the world went black, she could have sworn she saw a golden glow in the innkeeper's eyes.

CHAPTER EIGHTEEN

THE LIGHT OF Rivercene was slowly replaced by the stars of the Abyss. And along with them, the golden motes of Gaia's light drifted down to the hand laced between Vicky's fingers. Before Gaia had fully formed, her golden fingers flexed and warmed with the spirit of the goddess.

"Welcome back, little one. I thought it might be longer before I saw you once more." Gaia looked around the group. She eyed Terrence, but her gaze lingered on Zola. "You try to save him?"

"Ah'm willing to pay a price," Zola said. "But Ah do not want others to pay it for me."

Gaia inclined her head. "I am afraid you do not have a choice in the matter. It is not your sacrifice to make, nor should it be."

"Ask her," Zola said, looking to Vicky.

"Do you think you can do it?" Vicky didn't elaborate on the question. It was more of a test for Gaia, to see if the goddess could read her thoughts. Or if perhaps she had some other way of knowing what Vicky was going to ask. Luna's grip tightened on Vicky's shoulder.

"You are wise little one. But you must ask it of me here."

"Does that mean you already know what I'm going to ask you? You've heard the question before haven't you? You heard us at Rivercene."

A small smile traced the edges of Gaia's mouth, and a breeze that no one else could feel lifted her hair. "It is not what you think. I am not awake in that place."

Vicky tried not to look irritated. She had her theories, but Gaia obviously wasn't going to tell her what she wanted to hear at this point, and Vicky knew they had more pressing matters. "We need you to get us to the Obsidian Inn. We'll meet Drake there, and then … and then we face Damian."

"We only face Damian if we stop his sister," Zola said.

Vicky nodded. "And then we need you to bring Damian here." The words spilled from her mouth. She felt as if she didn't say them fast enough, Gaia would be more likely to say no. To say she couldn't go against her master like that. "It's to protect him."

For a time, Gaia didn't respond. Vicky had expected a protest, or even anger from the Titan. Not silence. She started to open her mouth, but Zola shook her head.

Vicky's heart pounded in her ears, and her patience wore thinner with every step.

Gaia looked away from Vicky, and studied something in the distance. "It is … possible. But I do not know if the compulsion laid upon me by the Mad King will keep me from doing as you ask."

"But you'll try?" Vicky asked. "We just need you to try."

"I shall. But I cannot act alone. It must be you, one who has dwelled in the Burning Lands. A being who lives on that channel of energy Damian Vesik carved through the Seal to pour into his own realm. You understand, you may not survive."

"What?" Zola asked.

"But he would?" Vicky asked. "Damian and Sam would survive?"

"It would not break the seal between brother and sister; only yours would be lost."

"No," Zola said. "Damian would never ask you to risk that. Ah don't care what the odds are, you can't do it. Even if you lived, the knowledge would kill them both."

"Then if something happens, you can't ever tell him." Vicky clenched her teeth together. "Tell him it was Nudd. Tell him it was a monster in the Abyss. I don't care. If I can save them, I'm going to do it."

Gaia frowned and turned her attention to Terrence. "You have a mighty bond with the forest gods. Are *you* willing to make the sacrifice?"

"Sacrifice?" Terrence asked.

"You are bound to this child as much as you are to the necromancer. The powers are intertwined, and I do not know if one can be separated without destroying the other's creations."

"I've been willing since the day I became a soldier."

"We need Terrence intact," Zola said, interrupting them. "The ghosts attached to a necromancer are like an anchor. They can pull him back from the edge, or at the very least give him something to hold onto."

Gaia inclined her head. "Let us hope that is enough for now. We are here." She swept her hand forward and Vicky shuddered when she saw the shadows out of the corner of her eye. Beside them on the golden path was the writhing mass of one of the lamprey creatures.

"What the hell are those things?" Vicky asked.

"The worms?" Gaia asked. "I cannot say with certainty. But I have long held the belief that they are spawned of the eldritch things and sometimes pulled through the Seals. I wonder if the Old Gods give them a channel, a way to break into realities to which they should not have access. But I am afraid if one was to learn the answer to that question, the very existence of this realm might end."

"Not much of a pep talk before a battle," Zola muttered.

Gaia smiled. "You have much the same humor as your pupil. You have taught him well, and he has done much good for it. Do not despair until all hope has left."

Zola tilted her head and exchanged a long gaze with the goddess before finally turning away.

"Are you ready?" Gaia asked, turning back to Vicky.

Vicky nodded, and Terrence cursed. Jasper trilled on Vicky's shoulder.

"I will await your call," Gaia said. "And this will end, no matter the cost."

Before Vicky could reply, Gaia released her hand, and they fell through shadow.

CHAPTER NINETEEN

VICKY HAD HEARD Damian complain about some of his exits from the Abyss on more than one occasion. She'd experienced trips through the Warded Ways of the fairies enough to understand how violent a trip those could be, but her experiences had never been quite so … nauseating.

Their fall turned into a spiral, as if a massive whirlpool had caught them in its current and whipped them around without mercy. That sensation suddenly reversed, and the world burst back into the light. Vicky barely had time to shout before her shoulder crashed into a stone wall and she stumbled backward.

Her head was still spinning when she looked up and took stock of her party. Zola leaned casually on her cane as if she were just on an ordinary trip and had simply stepped through a doorway onto a street.

Jasper's eyes spun in circles before he blinked and the black orbs stabilized. It looked like something out of a cartoon, and Vicky couldn't stop a small smile.

Terrence, on the other hand, leaned over in the corner, and Vicky swore the ghost looked green.

"Can ghosts puke?" Vicky asked. "I never puked when I was a ghost. Is that a thing?"

"Really not helpful," Terrence groaned out. "Really." Something echoed out of the ghost that sounded very much like a dry heave before he finally straightened and ran his hands down his cheeks. "That was horrible. That. Was. Horrible."

"I'm with Terrence," Luna muttered, leaning against Zola for a brief time before stretching her back.

"It's quiet," Zola said.

"Where are we?" Vicky asked.

Zola squinted down the hall. "We're near the entrance to the Obsidian Inn. That's the guard shack where the Utukku turn everything into a kebab." She frowned. "Come on. If Drake's not here, he may be in the training grounds. But if he's not there, we don't have time to waste. We need to find Sam, and to do that we might have to get behind enemy lines."

Vicky stuffed the hand of Gaia into the backpack while Terrence held it open for her. She zipped it up and took it from the ghost, keeping the makeshift strap slung crossways over her shoulder. "Let's go."

It didn't take long to reach the doors hidden in the stone. Behind them was the corridor that led to the intricately carved doors of the training hall. Vicky remembered the raucous sounds of the drilling Fae, and the fights in the circle, and the coordinated dance of the owl knights. But as the inner doors swung open, the Hall felt more like a tomb.

"Emptied out," Zola said, and there was a heaviness to her voice as it echoed around them.

"Did they retreat?" Terrence asked. "Did they all deploy to the battle?"

"Could be a mix."

"Some of them could've defected," Vicky said. "I ran into more than one owl knight."

Terrence looked around the Hall. "I saw them too."

They walked a little deeper into the cavern. A small armory off to the left caught Vicky's eye. She headed over to it and grabbed a thick rope off a shelf that only held a few small knives. She fed it through the fasteners on the backpack, and tied it as tight as she could before cutting the excess off with the knife. It wouldn't be the most comfortable thing in the world, but at least she could slide it over both arms again. The pack was heavy with all the ammunition, and Damian was going to need a new one when they got him out of this. *If* they got out of this. But Vicky didn't hold onto that thought. They'd either fix this, or it would be someone else's problem.

Footsteps echoed behind them, and a small knot of dread loosened just a bit when Vicky saw Drake stalking toward her.

The feeling didn't last.

"It's worse than we thought," Drake said. "The battle hasn't stopped. The Inn deployed in waves at Morrigan's order. They're holding Nudd's forces back, but it's just a matter of time."

"Time until what?" Zola asked.

"Until Damian kills them all. He already engaged one of the companies, and they didn't fare well. What I don't understand is why he's off to the northwest. Nudd clearly knows at this point that the Inn is here. Unless he knows something we don't. Or has some plan besides simply wiping out the Inn."

"If the battle hasn't stopped," Vicky said, "where did the reporters get that footage on TV?"

"Every battle has lulls," Drake said. "Nudd's not stupid. He knows those reporters are out there. He's going to keep them safe to broadcast his *glory*." Disgust dripped from Drake's words.

"Then we move," Zola said. "Now."

Drake studied Terrence. "Are you sure you want to bring the ghost into this?"

"Am Ah sure?" Zola asked. "You'd be mad not to. At the very least, Terrence is a barometer of Damian's powers."

Drake shook his head. "That doesn't matter. We have no way to tell if the power Damian imbued him with needs the necromancer's consciousness or not."

Zola narrowed her eyes. "You worry about lighting things up with your dragon. Let me worry about the hard stuff."

Drake stiffened at the snap in Zola's voice, but he didn't respond. Perhaps he had enough experience over the millennia to realize getting into an argument a few minutes before going to battle wasn't the best idea.

"I'm a damn good shot," Terrence said. "I can make use of my gun, much more than being a thermometer."

"Barometer," Zola said.

Luna snorted.

Drake nodded slowly. "That gun does seem to be channeling some of the necromancer's power."

"It blew apart one of those gravemakers well enough. Although the things always seem to come back together."

Zola rubbed at her chin. "That is unusually powerful for any magic. Keep it at the ready. Vicky, let me see that backpack." Zola muttered to herself as she unzipped the pack. Vicky felt a jerk, and Zola almost pulled her off her feet as the old Cajun lifted something out of the pack. When the backpack zipped closed, Vicky turned around and eyed the pepperbox in Zola's hand.

"Take it," she said, holding the old fairy-worked gun out to Terrence.

The ghost hesitated, then wrapped his hand around the butt of the gun. Runes lit up along the side of the barrel and down the trigger guard until the wood of the grips began to smoke. The runes glowed through Terrence's pale hand. "What is this?"

"A very unpleasant surprise for anything that gets in your way." Zola held out a few of the speed loaders to Terrence.

"I don't understand," Terrence said. "Even if I can shoot this thing, what are these for?" As he asked the question, he started dropping the speed loaders into an old satchel at his side. He hit the button on one of them, and the shells fell away, clattering down into the pouch. Terrence frowned at the empty speed loader and then dropped the mechanism in too.

"It doesn't load from the muzzle," Zola said. "It's modified. Load it from the breach."

Terrence fumbled with it and cracked the pepperbox open. His eyebrows rose slightly at the insanely intricate gear work that waited inside. "That's impossible."

"An old friend worked that gun over. It's precious to Damian. Don't break it."

Terrence pursed his lips and gave her a nod before he snapped the breach closed and fed the pepperbox through the belt at his waist. Vicky hadn't noticed the buckle before. Her dad had one like it, and she knew it was a Union buckle. But unlike the bent and decayed one her father had found, this had a bright sheen to it even in its semi-translucent state.

"I don't have anything in here for you," Vicky said, looking at Luna.

The death bat snapped her arm out, and the razor-like edge of her wing almost sang with the motion. "I'm good."

"It would be best if we can reach the front lines without being seen," Drake said.

"Oh, of course," Zola said. "It would also be best if Ah'd won the lottery ten years ago and retired to the Caribbean before any of this shit happened."

Drake blinked at the old Cajun. He couldn't see her face when she turned away. Couldn't see the small smile she gave Vicky, and the quick wink of her eye.

"Regardless, we have two reapers."

"Nudd has the Beast of Gorias," Drake said. "Her rider is skilled, and the cruel treatment of that reaper has turned it into an unpredictable enemy."

"At least we won't be bored today." Zola strode forward, her cane cracking on the stone of the cavern and echoing all around them. Two furry balls rolled across the ground at her heels, and Drake bowed his head briefly before following Zola into battle.

CHAPTER TWENTY

THEY WALKED A short distance before both dragons took their larger forms. They'd almost reached the courtyard with the basilisk bones before they could hear the far-off sounds of battle.

Vicky thought it was surreal, knowing fairies and friends were fighting to the death, but all they heard were booms and the occasional whisper of a dying scream. Closer to the horizon, where the new day's sun offered enough light, she could see small dots circling in the air, some falling to the earth, others rocketing into the heavens.

"There are far more forces in the sky now," Drake said. "The only other way to get close without being seen would be to take to the underground. But the reapers aren't as effective in enclosed space."

"Unless you just need to light up the hallway," Vicky said. "They're pretty damn good at that."

"That they are," Drake said, mounting his dragon and sliding between two curved spines on her back that acted as a saddle.

"Ah'll stay with Vicky," Zola said. "Whatever you can do to keep them off us, do it."

Drake inclined his head. "I will. You keep her safe. Keep her alive. Or we'll have words."

"No you won't," Vicky said, eyeing both of them in turn. "If I die, the only person you should be having words with is Gwynn Ap Nudd. And the only words should be a knife in his face."

Terrence cocked his head at Vicky as he followed her up onto Jasper's back. Zola was the last to join them, staying closer to Jasper's tail, though Vicky worried the ride might be a little less stable toward the rear of the dragon.

Zola saw her looking and said, "Ah'll be fine. Worry about your own ass."

"Best advice I've heard all day," Drake said. "Jasper." Drake waited for the dragon to look at him. "Anything gets near you, burn it out of the sky."

With that, Drake took to the air. The great dragon bore down with its wings and vanished into a low cloud bank.

"Let's follow them," Zola said.

Vicky patted Jasper on the neck, giving the signal. The dragon hunched down and launched himself into the air on powerful legs before his wings did the rest. It was an odd sensation, and one that Vicky didn't know if she'd ever get used to. The feeling of her heart falling into her stomach, like a small dip on a roller coaster. That made her think of Terrence's trip through the Abyss, and she couldn't stop a wicked grin.

Luna squinted against the wind, her ears flat against her head as Jasper picked up speed.

"How are we going to find her?" Terrence asked.

"Samantha?" Zola asked. "That's why Ah'm here. You might be a barometer of Damian's powers. But Ah could recognize that boy's soul anywhere."

Vicky looked back at the old Cajun. "What are you going to do?"

"You two are both tied to Damian. Even now, Ah can see the faint lines of power that tie you to him being stretched to the northwest. Though Ah can't see the boy, Ah can tell you exactly where he is. But what Ah expect will happen is that your tie to Samantha is going to pull you in a different direction. Two directions, to be exact. Whichever one Terrence isn't tied to will be where we'll find Sam."

Something unraveled in Vicky's chest. An uncertainty, even dread, that she hadn't fully realized the scope of. She hadn't really believed they'd find Sam, and that doubt had been so firm in her mind it churned her stomach. She hadn't believed they really had a chance to get out of this. But with Zola, maybe they did. The clouds closed around them, and a chill settled into her bones.

✦   ✦   ✦

VICKY'S VISION DIMMED as Jasper flew deeper into the cloud bank, and she could feel the coming storm. She had faith Jasper was following Drake and his dragon, but she couldn't see more than a foot in front of her face. The cloud seemed to go on forever, until they finally broke through the wall on the other side.

Not far ahead of them were the grayish brown wings of Drake's mount. Wind whipped the fairy's hair back, causing his plaited platinum braid to snap. The sun rose in earnest now, and it sent the wall of clouds behind them into a fiery cascade of light. In the distance, as they flew high above the walls and spires of Falias, fire of a different sort burned.

"By the gods," Zola said.

Even as the old Cajun spoke, Drake pointed to the distant carnage. It was hard to make out any details, but it wasn't hard to imagine what was happening. Bursts of fire and towering explosions of blue lightning followed a shadow around the edge of the city. As far out as they were, Vicky wasn't sure just how big what she was watching actually was. But those bolts, and that fire, had to be massive. How many people had died in each one of those eruptions? How many people had Damian killed?

Drake's dragon pulled up until the beast and her rider hovered just over Jasper. It was a maneuver Vicky had seen them do many times when they'd flown together. It gave them the perfect angle to shout down, so they could speak above the wind and occasional roar of their mounts.

"No doubt that is Damian," Drake said. "I haven't seen any flyers yet, but it's just a matter of time."

"There!" Luna shouted.

Something shifted in the corner of Vicky's eye. When she glanced back, she saw Terrence leveling his rifle. Aiming at Drake. "No!"

The report thundered around them. Drake pulled his dragon away, but he would have been far too slow if Terrence had been aiming for him. Instead, a tiny scream echoed out around them and wings with no body fluttered through the air past Vicky. Jasper opened his jaws and a blue fireball sent another charred corpse to follow the fairy into hell.

"A little warning next time," Drake shouted. He hesitated and added, "Much thanks for the well-placed shot."

Terrence ran his fingers along the barrel. "I always

did have good eyes. I guess they haven't failed me yet. I appreciate the tip, kid."

Luna grinned at the ghost.

"We'll definitely have to get you some chicken guts after this," Zola said. She reached up and grasped Terrence's shoulder. The ghost smiled as Drake's dragon swooped back in and hovered above them.

"If they have knights up here without their owls, they're going to be hard to spot. If Jasper gets spooked, follow his instincts. We'll probably see whatever's coming before you do. Unless it's coming from above and behind us." Drake said the last with a frown, no doubt reflecting on how much trouble he'd just avoided.

"I'm going higher," Drake said. "I see anything trying to ambush you, I'll take it out of the sky. Watch your backs regardless."

"You too." Vicky watched them rise, the pale gray underbelly of his dragon almost vanishing against the gray sky. She looked back at Zola and asked, "Which way?"

Zola pulled her hood back, her braids catching the wind as Jasper propelled them forward. Her eyes lost focus and Vicky could sense the change. Something shifted in the air around her, brushed against her aura, and called to her from the shadows she'd grown to be so familiar with.

Being able to feel someone else's aura was an unnerving thing. And even though Vicky knew it was
Zola, knew the old Cajun would do anything she could
to protect her, Damian, and Sam, it still felt like
walking through a massive cobweb.

"Just like a damn compass," Zola said, showing
Vicky a toothy grin. "They're moving fast, which is
good. Nothing's attacked them. But I'm afraid that
means nothing is slowing them down either."

"You don't think she's alone?" Vicky asked.

Zola shook her head. "Vik keeps closer tabs on that
girl than she knows. Sam went looking for a trip
through the Warded Ways, he would've known about
it."

Vicky frowned. She wasn't sure Zola was right
about that. Sam was resourceful, cunning, and if
anyone was going to outwit a centuries-old vampire,
Vicky wouldn't put it past Sam.

Jasper bent his head backward until he was upside
down and eyed the riders on his back.

"Can you see it?" Zola asked.

The dragon chuffed, a small puff of smoke rising
from the edges of his mouth before straightening his
neck out again.

"Follow the short one," Zola said, gesturing to

something Vicky couldn't see but which Jasper apparently could.

The dragon dove.

Vicky and Terrence grabbed the spines of Jasper's back and held on for dear life. Zola laughed, clearly exhilarated, and Vicky worried the sound was a little unhinged. But when Vicky glanced back, she saw the wind and rain turning the death bat into something that looked like a wet chihuahua in a wind tunnel. She barely choked back a laugh of her own.

"What's Jasper following?" Vicky asked, focusing on the view in front of them once more.

"It's like a pale soulsword," Zola said. "I'd be surprised if you couldn't see it too. But you have to open your aura, and that's not something I'm going to be teaching you right now."

"Like the hands of a compass?" Vicky asked.

"A bit. But a bigger circle in the middle, and that's you and Terrence. But from that circle, light reaches out toward Damian and trails off. But there's another line coming from you, a dimmer line, and that is reaching for Sam."

At the mention of her name, Jasper accelerated. It was one of the times Vicky was reminded that Sam and Damian had grown up with Jasper. He'd been their friend in the shadows, their guardian. And she wondered what kind of things he'd had to protect them from. Other than Barbies, of course.

They were close enough to the buildings of Falias now that Jasper had to dive and veer around the taller spires. As another massive form came into view on the ground, running beside a goliath clad in black shadow, the Beast of Gorias found them.

CHAPTER TWENTY-ONE

V ICKY HAD BEEN hit hard before, but the impact between the horned dragon and Jasper was like the collision of two small planets. Scales were scraped away from Jasper's hide, and horns along the beast's flank broke off as they dug into Jasper's flesh. Terrence fired at the helmeted rider. One of the shots glanced off the fairy's shoulder, another pierced his wing, but the rider barely flinched. Dragons roared and barked as they circled each other in vicious arcs, intertwining in a graceful but deadly dance. Jasper unleashed a hellish fireball that finally forced the Beast of Gorias to turn away and regroup.

"Get us to the ground!" Zola shouted.

Jasper dove, but the beast was already on their tail again. Literally. The other dragon chomped down, causing Jasper to screech in pain as teeth dug into his flesh. But the defensive spines along his back had done their job; one of them had impaled the Beast of Gorias in the roof of its mouth. The dragon pulled away again, and this time its rider unleashed a hail of three quick shots from his bow.

The first caught Zola's shield and shattered. The second sunk into Vicky's backpack, and the third, the one that should've hit her in the head, was caught by a shield from the heavens.

Drake's cry was the stuff of nightmares. He wasn't on his dragon anymore. Perhaps he had taken the idea from the fairy who had almost cut him down. But unlike those failed attempts, Drake was a Demon Sword. And he had magicks to rival the Lords of Faerie. Fire erupted around him. Not the magical blue flame of the dragons, but an intense inferno spun from the bowels of a volcano.

The Beast of Gorias pulled away, but the heat singed the dragon's flank, burned away the hair exposed on the rider's head, and blistered flesh as Drake's sword rang off the rider's helmet. The rider was fast. Impossibly fast. He had his own shield up in an instant, and parried Drake's second blow.

Vicky didn't see what happened next, as Jasper dove straight for the ground, Luna launching off his back ahead of them. Jasper barely pulled up in time to land upright, and Vicky's face smashed against the spikes she'd been holding. She grunted, but she didn't slow down either. She slid off Jasper's back, made sure

Zola and Terrence were following her, and sprinted after the shadows in the dark.

Jasper launched himself into the air and released one last fireball toward the horned dragon. It smashed into the other creature's rear leg, and the beast roared. On singed wings, the beast tilted and fled. But Drake's dragon fell from the sky, descending on the Beast of Gorias with its claws outstretched, claws that tore through the rider and sent the fairy to the earth in pieces.

Drake's dragon looped around upside down and swept up underneath him, catching the Demon Sword across the saddle spot between her spines. She came down gently beside Jasper and chased after the group.

"He's hurt," Vicky said, glancing back again even as she hurried after the sprinting shadows in front of them.

"Ah know," Zola said. "But we have to get to Sam. It's our only chance."

Another fireball exploded in the distance, lighting the area around them, and Vicky finally understood why the massive shadow running beside the vampire seemed so familiar.

"Aeros!"

The pair paused near a wall, turning to survey who was behind them.

"God damn it, girl," Zola shouted at Sam. "You *did* get away from Vik. And you, you giant pile of rocks, what were you thinking?"

Aeros blinked slowly at Zola. "I am thinking my friends need help, and so I am helping them."

"Sam," Vicky said. "Don't."

Sam pulled the black mask off her face, and Vicky could see her equally black hair framing sad eyes. "I want to try to talk to him. But if it doesn't work … if it doesn't work …" Her hand pressed over a small bump beneath her jacket. Vicky had little doubt that's where she was hiding the *splendorum mortem*.

"There's another way," Vicky said, holding a hand out to Sam.

Sam turned around and looked away. Vicky blinked as she realized how close they'd gotten to Damian. Which meant they were behind enemy lines. Which meant as soon as any of the dark-touched noticed them, they were in deep shit.

"Gaia can take him," Vicky said, the words pouring out in a rush as she lowered her hand. "You don't have to kill us. We get Gaia to take him into the Abyss. If nothing else, it buys us time. Time is all we have, Sam."

"You mean to kill him?" Aeros asked, the old god's eyes widening. He crouched down beside Sam. "Do not let the shadows take the light."

Sam took a few quick breaths through her nose, and turned back toward Vicky and Aeros.

"It's a chance, Samantha," Zola said. "It's a chance."

"Are you sure?" Sam asked, her voice cracking.

Zola gave one slow nod.

Sam blinked rapidly. "Then you have to try."

"Zola," Terrence said, drawing the attention of the others. Drake's dragon had crouched beside him, and Terrence was eye level with the fairy in the saddle. "I think Drake's in trouble."

Zola cursed and hurried over to the fairy, Luna close behind her. "The one thing we don't have is a goddamned healer. Aeros, can you get him to the Morrigan? Or any of the Fae healers?"

"The city is stone," Aeros said. "I can do what is needed. But might it not be best for me to take you to Damian?"

Vicky looked between Zola and Drake. "Don't let him die. We'll take care of Damian. Don't let Drake die. He's … he's my friend. Come on Sam. Let's go save your brother."

"I didn't really think you people could get more insane," Terrence said. "But your ability to prove me wrong is unsettling."

Vicky watched as Aeros gently lifted Drake's limp form from the back of his dragon. His chest rose and fell slightly at the edges of his armor. He was alive, but the pooled blood that ran out when Aeros tilted his body just a little was terrible. He might be alive for now, but not for long.

"Hurry," Zola said with a glance to Vicky. "As fast as you can. And don't fight anything if you can avoid it. Ah don't know how much time he has."

Aeros turned and Drake's dragon snapped back into its brown furball form. The pile of fur climbed up on the old god's shoulder as Aeros faced one of the massive stone walls, and the rock simply parted before him. Stone ground together and shifted out of the way, creating an arch just tall enough for the old god to walk through. Vicky couldn't help but smile at the small bump in the archway that gave Drake's dragon just enough clearance to squeeze past. As she watched, the stone closed around Aeros, and he started to sink into the ground.

"That is one odd subway," Zola said.

Vicky looked up at Zola. "Like how you got to my parents' house?"

Zola nodded as the rain started to fall in earnest. "That's right. It seems like a long time ago now, but it's only been a couple days." Zola shook her head. "Let's go." Even as she strode forward, her eyes stayed locked on the vampire behind Vicky. "Samantha."

Sam took a deep breath, gave Zola a quick nod, and started forward with the others. Jasper shifted restlessly on Vicky's shoulder. On the one hand, she thought it was good that he was staying in his small furball form. He'd be harder to detect, but he also wouldn't be able to shield them as quickly if another archer as good as the rider of the Beast of Gorias showed up.

That became the least of her worries as the shadows shifted, and the dark-touched came with them.

CHAPTER TWENTY-TWO

NEAR THE TOP of one of the spires of Falias stood an antlered form. Nudd watched as his weapon, his creation, laid waste to the forces of the Obsidian Inn. He had been working on these plans for centuries. It was why he'd struck up the alliance with the dark-touched, why he had been willing to go into a debt of favors with their lords. But it hadn't been until Cara introduced him to Damian that a new approach formed in his mind.

He'd manipulated the sons of Anubis as far back as Leviticus, before the fall of Atlantis. But not even the water witches were aware of that. Nudd liked to keep his influence subtle, to play with grand distractions while his true intentions developed in the darkness.

In one sweeping blow, Hern had been eliminated, and Vesik had been bonded to him. The necromancer never understood his own potential. The powers he'd shown would be pale compared to what would be wrought by Nudd once Vesik was fully consumed by his own powers and under Nudd's control. And he was close now. So close. A rare smile etched its way across the old Fae's face in the shadows of his helmet.

The only weakness his weapon had was Vesik's own sister, and the child who had been the Destroyer. And who would be willing to strike either of them down? But they'd shown themselves. What could that pair hope to accomplish? It was unfortunate he couldn't just kill them both to end their annoyance.

But now they'd brought themselves to him. He only needed to capture them, hold them where he could keep them alive. Where he could keep the weakness of his weapon at bay, and bring the commoners to heel.

It had been a long game, but his pledge to the dark-touched and their masters would be fulfilled.

Nudd watched the dark-touched flow into the courtyard around Samantha Vesik and the child who he still thought of as the Destroyer.

Footsteps crunched on the rooftop beside him. Nudd turned to find one of the dark-touched generals. "The battle goes well."

"Of course. This battle was fated to go well the moment Hern and Damian collided."

"Have you heard from the Demon Sword?" Nudd asked.

"A pawn you should not trust," the vampire hissed.

"Have you forgotten the path of the other Demon

Sword?" Nudd asked. "He was loyal to me until the day his mother died. And that is what you do not understand about the Fae. They are loyal to their core."

The dark-touched didn't answer immediately. "The time has come to fulfill your bargain, Lord Nudd."

Nudd didn't miss the slight. "The necromancer isn't mine, yet. Not fully."

"It would be simpler if you would allow us to kill them," the general said.

"If there is no other option, you will let them go. And no, I will not hesitate to sacrifice every last one of you if it repays my debt to your lords."

"You play with powers you do not understand."

Nudd let out a humorless laugh. "Oh, I understand. What you fail to comprehend is the point of the battle below you. This," he said with a sweeping gesture that encompassed the courtyard and the colossus beyond, "this is to drive out the last of Damian's humanity. And to that end, this battle is nearly won. The rest are mere jewels in a crown, and perhaps that your lords understand better than you, which is why you must do as I say at their order."

The dark-touched didn't respond, instead studying the scene unfolding below them. One of the dragons was still with the interlopers. Blue flame scorched the stone walls near the street, and the roars shook the spire they were perched on.

CHAPTER TWENTY-THREE

THE SKELETONS FOLLOWED the dark-touched. Vicky cursed as the shadows of Damian's cloak writhed through the walls around them, and the skeletons' empty eyes strode onto the field of battle. Even as they cut down the dark-touched, and the vampires wore them down in turn, more came.

Luna earned her name time and time again, the edge of her wings making short work of one vampire after another. It wasn't long before the dark-touched realized they were outmatched in a direct assault on the now blood-soaked puffball, and they focused on the dragon.

Jasper belched an orb of blue fire that blasted one of the skeletons apart and crashed into the edge of a shadowy cloak piece. The substance of it brightened momentarily before it floated away like ash in a strong breeze.

Vicky barely dodged the swipe of another dark-touched's claws. She didn't have time to dodge the next strike, but she didn't need to. Sam, moving impossibly fast, struck out at the things back. The vampire folded around the strike, and didn't move again. Vicky didn't understand what happened, until she saw the bloody blade of the *splendorum mortem* in Sam's hand.

"Jasper!" Vicky shouted. "Burn the cloaks!"

The dragon cocked his head, and Vicky realized he didn't understand. She pointed with the blazing soulsword in her right hand.

"The shadows where the skeletons are!"

That Jasper understood. He pulled his head back and his neck expanded before a hellish stream of blue fire scorched the stone and shadows and turned every inch of the cloaks they could see to ash. Some of the skeletons fell in the blast, a few managed to start putting themselves back together, but many collapsed to the ground unmoving.

It wasn't much, but it was something. Vicky lashed out with her soulswords, cutting away armor and blades and heads. On the opposite side of the court-yard, Zola's gray cloak snapped in the wind as the skies opened into a downpour. Water streamed over the Cajun's eyes, but it didn't slow her movements, or her magic. Lightning roared from the head of Zola's knobby old cane. Bolts crashed into the stone and cloaks and vampires alike. And wherever the bolts touched, only destruction remained. Flesh parted and exploded into charred masses, revealing the bones of the dark-touched. The vampires howled in pain, only to meet the end of Terrence's bayonet a moment later. He tried shooting a few of them, but whatever magic his gun had, it didn't penetrate the dark-touched helmets. It left scars behind, but still the things came at them.

Zola fell back, keeping Sam behind her as she fended off another skeleton that rode through the shadows on the back of a ghostly horse.

"We can't win this!" Zola said. "We go for Damian now, or we lose everything."

"Jasper!" Vicky snapped. "Launchpad!"

The dragon didn't hesitate. It was a command they'd worked on with Drake, and one that she'd thought silly at the time. But it didn't seem so silly now. The dragon flattened out and dove into the center of the group. Gray flesh and scales popped up between them all, snapping them up onto the newly formed dragon's back, much to the shouting protests of Zola, Luna, and Terrence. Vicky guessed she could have warned them, but it was too late now.

"Hold on tight!" Vicky shouted.

Jasper launched into the air, narrowly missing the claws of a dark-touched. The other vampires scrambled up the spires and towers around them. Vicky's heart sank as she realized how fast their pursuers were moving. If they got high enough, they could easily leap out onto Jasper. Vicky patted the dragon's neck and told him to get as high as he could.

Jasper's wings flexed and they rocketed forward. From the corner of Vicky's eye, as they passed one of the highest spires, she could've sworn she saw a shadowy form with antlers watching them. When she turned to look, there was nothing there. The first of the dark-touched leapt, but they were too high, and the vampire flailed as it fell back to the earth.

✦　　✦　　✦

THEY CLEARED THE wall, rain stinging their faces as Jasper hurtled at the colossus. The view opened up below Vicky, and the scale of the carnage was laid out before them. Empty Fae armor, shredded vampires, and a handful of what looked like commoners lay strewn across the ground. But even as the dead and dying sank into the mud around the shattered stones of Falias, Nudd's forces still fought. Every step Damian took blew apart another building, sending a shower of corpses out in a grisly silhouette against the lightning of the coming thunderstorm.

"Get me up to his face!" Sam shouted. "I want to

look him in the eye!"

Terrence shook his head. "No, get to his back, between the shoulder blades. That's where I saw him, that's where I got the pack."

Vicky watched in horror as something red and bright bulged near the shoulder of the colossus. It rippled and raced down the obsidian black arm until a fireball the size of her parents' home exploded from his fingertips. Water boiled in the impact, turning mud to brittle earth in a flash of hellish fire.

"I think staying behind him is an excellent idea," Luna shouted.

Sam didn't respond. Her eyes locked on the thing that was her brother, and Vicky knew the hollow look of loss. If Sam hadn't already lost hope, it was barely a flicker in the presence of this nightmare.

The colossus's hand turned palm up and swept underneath them. Vicky saw the light a split second before bolts of power erupted from Damian's fingertips. They lanced into the sky, Jasper narrowly avoiding the two nearest bolts, but the owl knights above the colossus had no such luck. Feathers and armor and screams flew in every direction as the scent of scorched flesh and hair filled Vicky's nostrils. Something slammed into Jasper next to her and left a bloody streak before it fell off into the chaos of the battle below.

"I can feel them," Terrence said with a grunt.

"By the gods," Zola said. "Terrence! Terrence, what the hell is happening to you?"

Vicky glanced back, catching of glimpse of Zola's wide eyes. Terrence wasn't the same pale translucence Vicky had become so accustomed to seeing. His edges flickered with red and black, the power of demons. Zola reached out to grab the ghost.

"No!" Terrence snapped. "Let me do this. I can reach him."

Sam drew the *splendorum mortem* from its sheath once more. "If he turns?"

"If he turns into what?" Zola said.

They both look confused, but they weren't watching the colossus. They didn't see the flesh of the gravemakers shifting on the giant's back. The colossus stumbled, and the black sludge of the corrupted armor split. The gap was huge, so deep she could see something like gold inside, as if the thing had been cut down to its very soul.

But it wasn't a nebulous light, or the piercing glow of a soulsword. It looked more like armor, or a person. But Damian wasn't that large. Hern wasn't that large. It was like something else had sheltered inside of their combined powers. A greater darkness, or a massive demon.

"I don't know how long I can hold it," Terrence said, and when Vicky glanced back again, the reddish black coloring had crawled down his forearms and up to his elbows. In a snap decision, she patted Jasper twice, smacked one of his spines, and the dragon twisted. Instead of a gentle turn around the colossus, Jasper rocketed to his back, crashing into the black mass, and digging his claws deep into the flesh as an anchor.

Screams echoed in Vicky's head, pained cries like a thousand people had been stabbed in one mighty blow. It was then she knew Terrence had been right. Damian was still there. But so were all the souls that had been trapped within him.

"Damian!" Sam said, her voice a cry in the thunder that surrounded them. "You're killing us!"

But the colossus didn't slow. He didn't acknowledge them. Instead, the black sludge of the gravemakers shifted toward them, roiling like scorched bark, forming hands to reach out to the dragon.

"Damian!" Sam screamed, her knuckles whitening around the *splendorum mortem*. Vicky's heart slammed in her chest as Sam raised the dagger.

The gravemakers froze, struggling to move, and golden light seeped through the cracks in their flesh, brightening into miniature suns.

Terrence leveled the gun at the nearest of them and fired. The bark-like flesh ruptured, white viscous fluid spraying out around the wound. Terrence took aim and pulled the trigger again, cutting down faces and arms and hands as fast as his finger could pull the trigger on the ghostly weapon in his hands.

Still, the things reformed and closed on them.

"He's losing it," Terrence said shaking his hand where it had turned into a sickly red hue. "It burns. Shit, it burns!"

Sam moved, the *splendorum mortem* clutched in her hand, and Vicky knew what was coming. She shouted, "Take my hand! Don't you dare strike him down! We are *not* dead yet!"

Zola climbed forward on Jasper's back, one hand locked around Terrence and the other on Sam's shoulder. "Take the chance, Samantha. Take her hand."

Sam glanced back at Zola. She turned to Vicky with tears in her eyes before she slid the dagger into its sheath and took the hand of the girl destined to be the Destroyer.

Vicky laced her fingers into Gaia's, and before the light had completely faded and the Abyss swallowed the skies, she screamed out, "We have him! Bring him with us!"

The world fractured around them.

The golden lights of the Abyss fell and shattered as if they were stained glass dropped from a cathedral window. Lines and ripples shot out all around, and through each Vicky saw a different sight. In one, she saw the body of Gaia beneath Rivercene. Another showed her the Morrigan, a spear piercing the Crow; she became the witch and obliterated a fairy in a cloud of darkness. Through a third she glimpsed a golden werewolf, the jaws of a dark-touched held open by its mighty claws, until at last the jaws gave out, and Wahya used the dark-touched's own teeth to cut its head from its body. The spray of blood gave way to another vision, the innkeeper, standing outside in a half ring of the green men. The golden light of the Abyss shone from her eyes.

It all came together as one mighty symphony of light and death and life. Gaia's body formed not in the blackness of the Abyss, but for a moment she stood in the shadows of the storm. A golden vision, wrapping her arms around Damian's corrupted form, and before the world went black, Vicky saw the horned king on the spire. And heard his cry.

Then the darkness took them.

CHAPTER TWENTY-FOUR

VICKY'S HEART HAMMERED in her chest. Too long the world remained in darkness. The stars of the Abyss should have been there, but instead she found a cold so deep it brought nothing but pain.

Gaia's reassuring warmth should have greeted her. Friends should have appeared beside her. All that greeted Vicky was darkness.

Panic rose.

It felt like an eternity had passed before the infinite blackness finally broke open and the lights of the Abyss ignited once more. The stars had never been so blinding.

The path beneath their feet did not light smoothly. It stuttered and started until at last it grew solid. Zola and Terrence and Luna and Sam were all there, with Jasper nestled against Sam's neck.

"It is done," Gaia said. "He is here."

When Vicky turned to the goddess, she saw the colossus behind her, as if Damian himself had become one of the leviathans of the Abyss. A slow-motion, slow-moving titan of destruction.

"What now?" Sam asked, and even though she had tightly controlled the emotions in her voice, Vicky still heard the crack. Still heard the fear bleeding through.

"You intend to gift your powers to him?" Zola asked.

"Do you think that could free him?" Vicky asked.

"He is in my realm now," Gaia said. "His power is strong in this place. He can reach the Burning Lands and the power of your world at once. There is a possibility, a hope if you will, that if I granted my powers to him he would be able to step away from the darkness that has restrained him inside that shell."

"I sense a but coming," Sam said.

"It could also kill him. And me."

"Then it's your choice," Terrence said. "That's a choice no one can make for you."

"It was a choice we made some time ago," Gaia said. "And we have had much time to dwell on it. Come what may."

"And if Damian dies?" Terrence started.

"We die," Vicky said, looking up at Sam.

"It's still a chance," Luna said with a nod, clearly shaking from their ordeal.

"I'm willing to die for him and you," Sam said to

Vicky.

"Those bound to him will die," Gaia said. "And you are bound by strong magicks, but they are not the strongest magicks. A blood knot can be transferred, or erased, if one were to find another anchor."

Sam shook her head. "That's all that's keeping Vicky alive. It's not acceptable."

"There are other magicks," Gaia said again.

Vicky turned and looked at the ghost. The red had almost completely left Terrence's form now. And even as she watched, it faded more, until he had returned to a normal blue-and-white translucence.

"What do we have to do?" Zola asked.

"Would you like to know?" Gaia asked, turning her attention back to Vicky.

"Yes, answer Zola's question. What do we need to do?"

"Very well," Gaia said. "I'm afraid I do not have all of the answers for you, but I know some of those who do. You will need Tessrian, rightful heir to the throne of the Burning Lands. Koda of the Society of Flame. And Hugh of the River Pack, guardian of the Heart of Quindaro."

"That's a new one," Zola said.

"I will watch over Damian here as I can. To make sure he is kept safe from the most dangerous of the

Abyss creatures."

"Like the leviathans?" Vicky asked.

Gaia shook her head slowly. "I would let him battle the leviathans on his own in this form. Perhaps not the one known as Croatoan, but most of them would be no match for what he has become."

"It's a shame we can't just turn him on Nudd," Zola said.

"Nudd's war has not stopped," Gaia said. "Even as we stand here in this place, the fight rages on, and your friends still battle for their lives."

"We need to get back," Vicky said.

Zola frowned. "We need to get Sam back to the Pit, and get the soul stone Tessrian calls home." She blew out a breath. "And we'll need the key of the dead if we're going to talk to her."

"We can't just let them die out there," Sam said. "Vicky's right."

"If either one of you die, or Damian dies, you all die. You risk too much." Zola's voice was almost pleading. And that fact clearly shook Sam. The vampire almost looked like Zola had slapped her.

"We don't abandon our brothers," Terrence said. "But I think you already know that." He gave Zola a small smile. "In fact, I'm sure of it."

Zola cursed. "If we are doing this, we're doing it my

way. We go in, we break the line, and we get everyone out we can. We're not there to try to overrun Nudd. The Obsidian Inn is not strong enough. As much as we'd like to imagine that Morrigan's forces have the power to take Nudd down on their own, they clearly do not. That was a goddamned army of dark-touched out there."

"Agreed," Vicky said. "Ready?"

"Then we go back," Sam said.

Terrence nodded.

"He will be safe with me," Gaia said. "When you're victorious, return here. I have found a safe place for you to rejoin the battle. But it may not remain safe for long."

"We're ready," Vicky said.

Gaia released her hand, and they fell from the Abyss.

CHAPTER TWENTY-FIVE

T HEY RETURNED TO the battlefield chaos in a brilliant flash of lightning and a boom of thunder. The rain had become a downpour, turning the landscape into a treacherous, slippery mess.

Shouts and incantations echoed in the distance as allies retreated—a stuttering horn sounding that call—but Nudd's soldiers were slow to follow. Vicky wondered if Nudd's forces had lost their direction when Damian was snatched away.

"Where the hell are we?" Vicky asked as her foot slid out of a shallow pool of mud.

"Look at the ghosts," Zola said.

Vicky eyed the still forms across the field of battle. They weren't marching as one anymore, and many of them stood stock still at attention, as if they'd been frozen there since the first battle of Gettysburg.

"It was all Damian?" Terrence asked.

"We can worry about that later," Zola said. "Right now we need to help end this battle."

"What battle?" Vicky asked as the shouts faded and the incantations lessened in the distance. "I don't hear much."

She could make out a few echoed screams, and the clanging of metal hitting stone. But there were no great magicks being thrown around. No dark-touched vampires rushing them from the shadows, and not a single skeleton or sliver of gravemaker to be seen.

"Jasper," Zola said. "Get us into the sky. We need to figure out where we're at."

Lightning crashed above them, and Vicky wondered just how good of an idea it was to go flying into a thunderstorm. She supposed they were going to find out.

She helped Jasper off her shoulder, and the furball erupted, his four legs exploding out and digging deep into the mud, cracking stone as his claws dug in. Jasper's tail swished and then stilled when Zola grabbed one of the spines and climbed up. She in turn offered Terrence a hand. Vicky hopped up to Jasper's knee and bounced to his back in a smooth, practiced motion. Luna remained silent, following Vicky's path and bouncing up onto the dragon's back.

"No need to show off, you two," Zola said.

Zola didn't poke fun at Sam as she reached forward and patted her shoulder. She had an understanding of what was on Sam's mind. Vicky had no doubt.

"He's really gone," Sam said.

"Yes," Zola said. "You're still here, and Vicky's still alive. Some part of him is still in there."

Sam nodded slowly as Jasper flexed his wings and took to the sky. "Then we'll do what we can."

They cleared a long, low stone building before Vicky could see the wall. Judging by the spires in the distance, it didn't take her long to figure out where they were, but it was still a jarring site to see the Western Wall blown out. Parts had fallen into the city, crushing buildings and gods knew how many Fae as something had forced its way in.

But other parts had been blown outward, and the flashes of lightning glinted on the steel of armor and swords long-vacant of the bodies they once shielded. That wasn't all that moved among the rubble. Shadows stayed close to the ground, hurrying from one patch of deep darkness to another, invisible outside of lightning bursts and carefully controlled *illuminadda* spells that lit and vanished like fireflies.

Zola's voice was barely a whisper. "Utukku."

Vicky had never heard of an Utukku raising arms for Nudd. She'd only seen them as allies of Nixie, and members of the Obsidian Inn. She tapped on Jasper's neck and pushed one of his spines toward the rubble.

The dragon turned gradually and swept down, lifting his tail to avoid hitting remnants of the stone wall before he settled to the muddy earth in silence.

The shadows had all vanished but one. A single hooded form stood at the edge of the ruins. Vicky pulled her hood back, and Zola said, "Thank the fucking gods." The old Cajun slid off Jasper and walked toward the Utukku. "How bad?"

"It has been bad, Zola Adannaya." She looked up at Vicky before returning her gaze to Zola. "What has become of the creature once named Damian Vesik?"

Zola sighed. "We're all safe. For now. Do you need help?"

In the lightning, Vicky could see the purple flesh of Uttuku's inner lid slide over her eye before slowly revealing it once more.

Utukku stuck the staff in her hand into the earth. "We are taking what we can for resources. There is much armor and weaponry buried in the rubble. Aeros helped us recover who we could, but I fear it was not many."

"Aeros," Zola said, her words hurried. "You know where he went? He had Drake with him, the Demon Sword, and he was gravely injured."

Utukku inclined her head. "To the west, you will find Morrigan's encampment. The healers have all been summoned there. If your friend is alive, you'll find him there."

"Thank you," Zola said. "Should you need us, you only have to ask."

Utukku smiled, though the expression was sad even on the reptilian face. "It is why we fight with necromancers at our side. Thank you."

Zola climbed onto Jasper's back with a helping hand from Terrence. Jasper didn't wait for a signal. He leapt off the ground and they sailed away from the walls of Falias, headed for the distant lights of Morrigan's camp.

✦   ✦   ✦

FOR ALL THE rubble and chaos they left behind in the wreckage to the northwest of Falias, Morrigan's camp was organized, tight, and well-protected. Zola almost missed the shimmer in the air. With only a split second to spare, she shouted, "Hit the ground, now!"

Vicky threw her arms around Jasper's neck, and the dragon responded in an instant. Instead of their continued path, the dragon pitched his wings forward and they dropped like a rock. Some fifty feet they fell from the sky, only to have Jasper spread his wings at the last moment to soften the landing. But even then Zola and Sam shouted as the car wreck-like impact shook them to the bone.

"What was that for?" Sam asked.

"That was so we didn't hit their shield at 60 miles an hour and go crashing to the earth from the back of the dragon."

Jasper reached out with his snout, sniffing at the air, but when he reached a little too far, an explosion of blue lightning singed his face and the dragon reared back with a barking cry. Terrence tumbled away in an awkward cartwheel, and that left Zola to hang on to a spine by the tips of her fingers.

"As I was saying," Zola said through gritted teeth before dropping to the earth. "It's well-guarded."

"Sam?" A voice echoed around them. "Sam!"

Vicky couldn't see who it was at first, until Zola cast an *illuminada* spell. The black and white Atlas moth pattern of the approaching wings came to life, and a silver-armored Fae stood staring at the dragon and his riders.

"Foster?" Sam didn't say anything more. She hopped off Jasper's back and ran to the fairy.

"Wait wait wait," Foster said waving his hands. "Drop the shield!"

Whoever Foster had shouted at formed a gateway in the shield a second before Sam plowed into the fairy. She wrapped her arms around him as if he was the last sane thing on the planet.

"Come on," Foster said as he gestured at the rest of the group while being strangled by Sam. "Get inside the barrier. We need to lock it down again."

Jasper snapped into his furball-sized form, shook some of the mud off his fur, and then politely deposited the rest on Vicky's shoulder. She grimaced at the cold squishy feeling, but figured the rain would take care of it soon enough.

Foster and Sam stayed still for a time. Luna looked up into the rain, her nose twitching along with her ears.

When Zola had enough of waiting, she asked, "Have you seen Aeros? Did Drake survive?"

Sam pulled away from Foster and turned around to face the rest of the group, wiping her cheek on her shoulder before giving Vicky a small smile. Even in the rain, the redness of her eyes revealed the tears.

"He's here," Foster said. "It was a near thing. Aeros almost got the both of them killed when he exploded into the middle of Morrigan's command tent."

Zola blinked.

Vicky looked at the old Cajun. "Well, you did tell him to find Morrigan."

Zola muttered under her breath. "The rock always had a gift for being a bit too literal."

ERIC R. ASHER

"Aideen?" Sam asked.

Foster smiled. "She's okay. Once the lines broke, she came back here. She's been working with the healers ever since. What happened to Damian?"

"We did," Vicky said. "I guess, more accurately, Gaia did."

Foster glanced between Zola and Sam. "Is he ..." But the fairy couldn't finish the question. His gaze trailed back to Vicky.

"He's safe," Vicky said.

"Can you take us to Aeros?" Zola asked. "Do you know where he is now?"

Foster blew a short series of whistles that sounded like a songbird. Someone echoed him back and Foster nodded. "Let's go."

The blood and mud closer to the barrier gave way to spongy grassland. And what had looked like simple small tents, almost like the plain canvas of an old army, resolved into massive structures, some of which had to have been nearly a city block long. Up close Vicky could make out the intricately sewn battle scenes and celebrations embroidered in a thread just slightly darker than the rest of the fabric.

"They're beautiful," Vicky said, running her hand along the edge of one of the tents.

"Yes, they are," Foster said. "They're meant for

celebrations, coronations, but not battlefields."

"Battles often result in one or two of those events," Zola said.

Foster gave her a wry smile before he pulled the flap of the tent in front of them open, and ushered the group inside a room not unlike a cathedral hall. Only this hall was longer, and filled with cots and explosions of white that didn't give off nearly as much light as they should. Rows upon rows of healers worked at the cots, and in the distance, Vicky could hear the cries of the dying, the ones the healers couldn't save.

"This feels familiar," Terrence said.

Foster nodded.

Vicky squinted in the direction Foster gestured and blinked in surprise she realized that the reinforcement at the base of one of the massive tent poles was actually the old god with his knees drawn up and his arms resting in his lap. As they drew closer, the golden green and yellow glow of the old god's eyes landed on their party.

"You're alive," Aeros said, his voice filling the tent and bringing most of the beds and fairies in the vicinity to silence.

"Mostly," Zola said. "Flying around on that dragon makes me feel like I'm three hundred."

"You got Drake here in time?" Vicky said, still

hesitant to believe the news Foster had already delivered them.

Aeros nodded, the granite of his head and neck grinding together with the motion. He turned slightly and held his hand out to reveal one of the beds. Black and white wings hung over the side, and the bandaged chest moved up and down, but the fairy didn't stir.

"It was a near thing. I don't know that he thought he was going to survive. He asked me to give you his armor if he didn't. Said you'd grow into it."

For the first time since the battle had begun, Vicky's façade cracked. She felt her lip tremble, and clenched her jaw, trying to lock the emotions down like she'd done so many times before. But there were times, when the weight was too much, when the relief at a pause in her nightmare caught her off guard, and she couldn't stop the tears.

Sam reached out, put an arm around her, pulled Vicky's head to her chest, and held her there as thunder boomed above them and the rain beat a staccato on the tent.

CHAPTER TWENTY-SIX

VICKY WASN'T SURE how long they'd been there when a strong hand gripped her shoulder. She lifted her head and smiled at the wrinkled old man before her. Most wouldn't believe that the kind smile and diminutive form behind the thick glasses hid the towering form of Wahya, the golden wolf.

"Little one," Wahya said, his voice soft, warm, and utterly reassuring. "You've done well. I am glad to see you all safe."

"Caroline?" Vicky asked.

Wahya frowned and tilted his head. "She will survive. She may be grumpy for a while, but she will survive. We plan to return to Antietam with Utukku. It's possible Nudd's soldiers have not found all of the vaults. If there are any artifacts remaining, we would prefer to claim them for ourselves.

"I have to talk to Hugh about saving Damian."

Wahya leaned against Drake's bed. "What makes you think they'll have an answer for you?"

"Gaia," Vicky said.

"The bloody Titan," Terrence muttered. "A *Titan*." He shook his head.

"Perhaps she has finally chosen her side," Wahya said. As if that made any sense to any of them. "She would be a powerful ally."

"I think she already is," Vicky said. But she didn't say it out loud, didn't say what she'd seen at Rivercene, the golden glow in the innkeeper's eyes that matched Gaia's in every way.

"I don't think I should leave him here," Vicky said, looking at Drake.

"He'll be safe here," Foster said, hopping up on the foot of the bed beside Wahya. "Aeros told us what happened. Told us he fought the Beast of Gorias. I would have to explain to you the last thousand years of Faerie history for you to understand how much that says. What you need to know is that Drake and the rider of the beast were once inseparable. For him to strike that fairy down ..." Foster shook his head. "I'm sorry I doubted you."

Vicky smiled at Foster. "Sometimes doubt is all that keeps you alive."

"Ah need to get back to Death's Door," Zola said, stretching her back and patting Aeros on the knee. "There are too many who know of the old chest." She said this in a hushed voice, barely loud enough for Vicky to hear her even though she was standing right next to her.

"I can escort you if you would like," Aeros said.

"Ah can take the Ways. There are enough fairies here that someone will open a portal for me. But Ah'd ask of you another favor, rock."

"Of course, old maid," Aeros said, his boulder-like face fracturing into a grin.

"Take Terrence back to Greenville. He's the strongest tie we have to Dirge. And Ah'm afraid before this is all over, we're going to need all of the forest gods on our side."

"That's it," Terrence asked. "I just go to Greenville and live my death?"

"Ah doubt very much you will be that fortunate," Zola said. "Stay with Dirge. Help him if you can."

"Come with me, Samantha," Zola said, dragging the vampire to her feet. "Let's get you home. Ah'm sure Vik will be very interested to hear the story of what you've been up to."

Sam gave Zola a nervous smile.

"Can I ride with you?" Vicky asked, looking at Aeros and Terrence. "I'd like to see Terrence home."

"Of course," Aeros said.

Wahya put his arm around Vicky's shoulder. "Until we meet again, little one."

She threw her arms around the old wolf, and crushed him in a hug.

Luna hugged the old wolf too as he turned away, and he scratched her between the ears.

"See you soon, kid," Foster said.

"Bye, Sam," Vicky said, hugging the vampire. "Try not to kill us, yeah?"

Sam squeezed her back.

"That's safe with me now," Zola said, patting a fold in her cloak. "You don't worry your head about that none. We've talked some sense into that vampire."

Vicky stepped away and smiled at Sam and the old necromancer as Aeros approached her. The stone of the Old God surrounded them, feeling like a slightly hard couch as Aeros folded over them and everything went dark.

A few minutes into the insane ride of bumps and sudden turns, and whatever else Aeros was doing to them as they flew beneath the earth, Vicky realized this was *very* much like a roller coaster.

✦　✦　✦

ONCE THEY WERE out of the city and away from foundations and the massive stones of Falias, the ride smoothed out. After a time, the cracks and joints around Aeros began to glow, and the pale green and yellow light accompanied them for the rest of the time underground.

"What are you going to do?" Terrence asked.

Vicky sighed and leaned against Jasper as he alternated purring and snoring. "Whatever I have to."

"Hugh and Quindaro are both in Kansas City," Luna said. "You'll have to go there."

Vicky took a deep breath, but she didn't answer.

"What's wrong?" Luna asked.

"There's too much in Kansas City," Vicky said. "The werewolves, the blood mages, the witches, and Camazotz."

"You'll have allies there."

Terrence shifted and rubbed his neck. "You need more than that. You need friends."

"They *are* more than that," Vicky said, her voice quiet against the rumble of Aeros's movement. "They're family."

Terrence gave her a small smile and patted the top of her shoe. "Even better."

"Almost there," Aeros said, the words filling the small chamber around them. "Hold on. We're going to shift directions."

Regardless of the warning, Luna squawked as she lost her balance at the sudden shift and crashed into

Vicky. Jasper vibrated with irritation as the pair smashed into him, waking him up as they all finally landed on Terrence in a tangled pile.

The ghost cursed, but the exclamation broke down into a laugh as they slowly righted themselves and the shadows of the underground were washed away in the morning light of the ruins of Greenville.

Terrence hurried out of the crater in the ground as Aeros lifted them up.

"That was nice," Luna said, stretching as she stepped out of the old god's shadow.

"Thank you," Vicky said, running a hand across Aeros's forearm.

"Terrence," a voice boomed. "I was concerned."

Terrence smiled. "I'm okay. I'm home."

"Oh wow," Vicky said, her eyes trailing up the trunk-like legs of the forest god, the vines forming his joints, and finally the jagged, glowing slashes in the bark that formed his face. "I thought you'd be like Stump."

Dirge cocked his head to the side. "I am, somewhat, like Stump."

"You're bigger. A lot bigger. Even bigger than Whip."

The forest god turned his focus to Vicky and crouched. "You are tied to Terrence." His eyes followed a thread no one else could see. "I thought only the necromancer could do that."

"He did," Vicky said. "I'm tied to Damian, so I think, through that link, Terrence is tied to me."

"Then I hope it will keep him in this plane longer than he would have otherwise stayed." Dirge turned to Luna. "And you, death bat. You have spent many days in these woods. I remember you, and the family you kept here."

Luna eyed the forest god before gesturing to the tree line. "Your forest looks healthier. I was worried after I heard a storm had hit here."

Dirge looked at the forest and his harsh expression softened to a smile. "I am well. Thanks greatly to your necromancer."

"He is with Gaia now," Aeros said. "Your goddess protects him."

"As she should," Dirge said. "He is a bringer of both life, and death. Perhaps more balanced than the commoners themselves in that way."

"An interesting theory," Aeros said. "Though I suspect the number of times I have used the word *unhinged* with Damian Vesik would make me feel otherwise."

"Order through chaos," Dirge said. "You can always find order in the chaos. Come, Terrence. Say hello to the others who dwell here."

The forest god reached out with a gentle cluster of bark and vines before Terrence held up his hand. "A minute."

He hurried over to Vicky. "No matter what happens, you've done more than anyone thought possible. If you need me …" he hesitated and glanced at Dirge. "If you need *us*, you need only send word."

Vicky hugged the ghost. Jasper chittered at Vicky's heels as Luna said goodbye too.

Dirge walked with Terrence, sparing only a single glance back as he said, "I fear this war has much life left to take."

"I need to get to Kansas City," Vicky said. "The innkeeper said Hugh has answers I need." She looked to Luna. "You coming with?"

"Wouldn't miss it. And I'm ready to get away from Rivercene for a bit."

Vicky nodded. "Aeros?"

"Not today, little one. Today I must return to Saint Charles. I suspect I know what Zola intends to do, and she would be safer if she had a shield."

"You're the best shield I can think of," Vicky said.

Jasper made an irritated squeak.

"Except for you, furball. Except for you."

"Be safe, Elizabeth Gray. Gwynn Ap Nudd still

walks this earth." With that, Aeros sank into the grass without crushing a single flower.

Vicky frowned at the empty grass and crossed her arms. "My name is Vicky." She shook her head. "Let's go."

Jasper exploded around them, crushing a great many flowers, before leaping into the air and carrying them toward Kansas City.

Note from Eric R. Asher

Thank you for spending time with the misfits! I'm blown away by the fantastic reader response to this series, and am so grateful to you all. The next book of misadventures is called *The Book of the Claw*, and it's available soon (or maybe now because I'm lazy about updating these things).

If you'd like an email when each new book releases, sign up for my mailing list (www.ericrasher.com). Emails only go out about once per month and your information is closely guarded by hungry cu siths.

Also, follow me on BookBub (bookbub.com /authors/eric-r-asher), and you'll always get an email for special sales.

Thanks for reading!
Eric

The Book of the Claw

The Vesik Series, book #10

By Eric R. Asher

And here's that excerpt we talked about!

Days Gone Bad

The Vesik Series, book #1

You are cordially invited to the wedding of

Elizabeth Berry

and

Michael William Wagner

On the twenty third of April, two o'clock

The Jewel Box in Forest Park

RSVP ...

"**B**LAH, BLAH, BLAH ..." I groaned and set the invitation down. "Sam's going to have an aneurysm over this one."

I walked to my old green fridge, popped the cap off a bottle of ale, and started scrounging for some food. I pressed a few buttons on my personal chef, a.k.a. microwave, and turned on the television. It was depressing. Every station was running the latest Amber Alert, flashing the picture of a missing girl with huge blue eyes and the devil's smile. Hopefully this girl gets a happy ending. The last two sure as hell didn't. I turned the set off and waited for my gourmet dinner to finish cooking. My phone rang about ten minutes later, interrupting a freshly microwaved chimichanga.

"Damn, that was fast." I let the phone ring a few times while I shoveled in a forkful of chimichanga and leaned back on my battered leather couch. My eyes passed over the outdated wood paneling on my ceiling and walls, taking in the meager light from two small lamps while I swallowed my dinner.

"Hello?" I said with the phone a good four inches from my ear.

"That, that, that … *bitch!*"

I stabbed the fork into my chimichanga and set the plate on my oversized oak coffee table. "Hey, Sam. You got Beth's invite."

She snarled something I couldn't quite make out.

I put the phone between my shoulder and ear, and slowly persuaded the coffee table to come closer. "Can I get the English translation on that?"

Sam puffed into the phone and said, "Don't start."

It was impossible to stifle a chuckle. I could just see her lips curling back and her black hair framing the rage on her face as she yelled into the phone.

"Thanks, Damian. Some brother you are."

"I'm getting the guilt loud and clear. Where's the spite?"

"Ah ha … ha … ha. Ass. I just can't believe it. She was my best friend! She sent the invite less than a week before the wedding! I can't *believe* that bitch is marrying my old boyfriend."

"You did die, you know."

"Not. Helping."

"Sorry, sorry. Look, I never had any real issues with Beth, she was always nice and—"

"Shut. Up. Damian. You're just saying that because she slept with you."

My jaw slackened in mock offense. "Oh, come on sis, it was only one time and—"

"I repeat, she slept with you."

I took another oversized bite of chimichanga before I said, "Comf omf Samf." I swallowed. "I was a teenager, what was I supposed to do?" Beth was, well, she was a valley goth girl when we were kids. Total wannabe, and the instant my sister told her I could see the occasional phantasm and sometimes hear the dead talk, Beth was all over me.

Sam's exasperation came over the phone in a puff of static.

"I take it you won't be giving a toast?"

Sam's breathing evened out. "Maybe, maybe I'll tell the guests about the time Beth accidentally slept with Mister Brown—"

"The math teacher?"

"—right before I turn the whole *effing* wedding party into vamps, or, or, give me a minute, I'll come up with something good. I'll do something horrible to her wedding. I'll make it the worst wedding day anyone could imagine. I want it to rain frogs while zombies rise up behind the wedding party and, hell, you just better buy the tux insurance."

I choked on a mouthful of ale and blinked at the phone a few times through watering eyes. "You want to know something, sis?"

"What?"

"Ale burns like a bitch when you shoot it through your nose."

She burst into laughter.

"Glad I could help." I rubbed my cheek while my brain scrambled for a way to defuse my sister, the vampiric time bomb. I knew she wasn't going to let it go and I couldn't even nudge her mind in a different direction over the phone.

"So, Demon, are you in? You could bring some zombies. It'll be a whole new spin on wedding crashers."

My eyes glanced down at the invitation as I wiped the ale off my nose. Forest Park, eh? There were a few interesting things I could do there. Art Museum, Zoo, pigeons, all kinds of trouble. I grinned, and I'm sure it was an evil grin. "Tell you what, leave everything to me. I'm not going to kill her husband to be, much to your disappointment, I'm sure, but I'll make it memorable. Consider it an early birthday present."

Silence.

"How about it, Sam?"

She sighed. "Alright, but if you don't make it good, I'll wrap that bitch up as a present for my new brothers to eat."

I stared at the receiver and wondered for a second if my sister was joking. I laughed nervously as my chimichanga curdled in my stomach.

Grab the first Vesik Box Set on Amazon today!

Also by Eric R. Asher

Keep track of Eric's new releases by receiving an email on release day. It's fast and easy to sign up for Eric's mailing list, and you'll also get an ebook copy of the subscriber exclusive anthology, *Whispers of War*.

Go here to get started: www.ericrasher.com

The Steamborn Trilogy:

Steamborn

Steamforged

Steamsworn

The Vesik Series:

(Recommended for Ages 17+)

Days Gone Bad

Wolves and the River of Stone

Winter's Demon

This Broken World

Destroyer Rising

Rattle the Bones

Witch Queen's War

Forgotten Ghosts

The Book of the Ghost

The Book of the Claw*

The Book of the Sea*

The Book of the Staff*
The Book of the Rune*
The Book of the Sails*
The Book of the Wing*
The Book of the Blade*
The Book of the Fang*
The Book of the Reaper*

The Vesik Series Box Sets

Box Set One (Books 1-3)
Box Set Two (Books 4-6)
Box Set Three (Books 7-8)
Box Set Four: The Books of the Dead Part 1 (Coming in 2020)*
Box Set Five: The Books of the Dead Part 2 (Coming in 2020)*

Mason Dixon – Monster Hunter:

Episode One
Episode Two
Episode Three

*Want to receive an email when one of Eric's books releases? Sign up for Eric's mailing list.
www.ericrasher.com

About the Author

Eric is a former bookseller, cellist, and comic seller currently living in Saint Louis, Missouri. A lifelong enthusiast of books, music, toys, and games, he discovered a love for the written word after being dragged to the library by his parents at a young age. When he is not writing, you can usually find him reading, gaming, or buried beneath a small avalanche of Transformers. For more about Eric, see: www.ericrasher.com

Enjoy this book? You can make a big difference.

Reviews are the most powerful tools I have when it comes to getting attention for my books. I don't have a huge marketing budget like some New York publishers, but I have something even better.

A committed and loyal bunch of readers.

Honest reviews help bring my books to the attention of other readers.

If you've enjoyed this book, I would be very grateful if you could take a minute to leave a review. It can be as short as you like. Thank you for spending time with Damian and the misfits.

Connect with Eric R. Asher Online:

Twitter: @ericrasher

Instagram: @ericrasher

Facebook: EricRAsher

www.ericrasher.com

eric@ericrasher.com